MOUNTAIN WARRIOR

By

Raland J. Patterson

Chapter 1

It was the fall of 1949, the day after Labor Day and the first day of school for kids in the North Georgia Mountains. It was Bill Carpenter's first day of school. He was beginning the first grade at Epworth Elementary.

"Momma, I'm six years old, you don't need to walk me to Mr. McGill's Grocery Store. I can get on the school bus myself." He pointed toward the store, "You can see the bus stop from right here. It's a long walk, and besides, you've got to milk the cow."

She knew he didn't want the other kids to think he was a baby needing her help, "Okay. Give me a kiss."

After the kiss, he shot out the front door of their house and ran on the trail by the barn. The barn was about halfway to McGill's. She stood on the porch and watched him, feeling pride in his independence. She could see he wasn't afraid of going to school, but was more afraid of seeming weak to the other kids. From the porch she could see the road that led past the grocery store. In a matter of minutes she saw him reach the clustered group of kids standing around the gas pumps

She turned and went back into the house to finish her chores, trying hard not to notice how quiet the house was without the constant chatter of her little man.

Bill was enjoying the ride to Epworth. He'd never been there before and when he saw the brick high school he couldn't believe his luck; that he'd actually be going to school in that building.

Epworth High School

As the bus passed it and stopped in front of a large, faded white wooden building, he felt slightly disappointed.

He followed the other students into the hallway, trying his best to blend in and look like he knew what he was doing. One of the older girls from the bus stop leaned over and pointed at a nearby door, "Bill, that's Miss Laura Water's first grade classroom. Go in there. She's a wonderful teacher."

Bill didn't even blink, but walked into that room like he owned it. As they entered, the teacher called out, "Take your seats and we'll get started."

As she wrote down their names, sometimes she'd say a name and ask if they were related. Bill listened closely and couldn't believe it when he realized she'd taught five of the kids' parents. She must be the oldest woman in the whole entire world!

When lunch came, she had all of them stand, get in line and then she led them across a field behind the large brick building. On the right side was another wooden building that was two stories tall. The teacher pointed up the stairs leading to the second floor and said, "Our principal and his family live up there." As they entered a large room, Bill could smell wonderful aromas and realized he was hungry.

They were told to line up next to the wall. A lady sitting at a table was collecting money. It scared Bill at first and then he remembered his mother had placed coins in the bib of his overalls. When he reached her, he unbuttoned the top of his bib and pulled out his change. She took the money, removed what she needed and handed the rest back to him, saying, "Keep the rest for tomorrow."

Bill ducked his head and grinned shyly, "Yes, ma'am."

Her lips twitched as she said, "You're welcome, young man."

He watched closely as the kids in front of him in line took a metal tray and grabbed silverware and started sliding their trays forward. He watched as the workers filled the plates with steaming hot food and handed it to each student. At the very end, each kid got a little bottle of fresh milk. As he was checking it all out, he realized he knew one of the ladies behind the counter. She went to his church! He quickly moved up to get his tray and went through the line like he'd done it a million times. At first he just stared at the bottle of milk – it was smaller than a baby's bottle. As he tasted the food, he nodded in satisfaction. He was going to like this school stuff just fine.

At the end of the day, he walked to the buses and saw the same girl standing in front of one the buses. As soon as she noticed he'd seen her, she climbed on without saying a word. Bill ran to the bus and moved quickly to the back. When the girl got off the bus at McGill's Grocery, he followed her, gave her a quick wave and began to run home. His mother was waiting on the porch. She had to smother her laugh because he was talking before he even reached her, saying, "Did you know Mrs. Loudermilk from church works in the lunchroom? She filled my plate with lots of good food. They have these really little bottles of milk. Did you know that?" She just smiled and let him talk. After listening to him for as long as she could, she said, "Let's take this inside. I need to get the table set. Your Daddy will be home soon and he likes to eat as soon as he gets here."

Bill just kept talking. "My teacher is Miss Laura, and she's really old. She's even older than Mamaw Carpenter. She's nice, but not as nice as Mamaw, though." mom just laughed and shook her head as he continued to babble. His telling her about his classroom reminded her she needed to thank Clara Jean for her help. He could never know they'd hatched a plan to take care of him weeks ago.

When Bill's Dad came through the door, Bill began to share his stories immediately. As usual, his Dad didn't give him any response and just sat down and ate. When Bill had finished recounting his entire day, his Daddy asked, "What's your bus driver's name?"

The question caught Bill off guard. He didn't have a clue and had no response to the question. His Daddy went back to eating and there was total silence for the remainder of the meal. That night after Bill had gone to sleep his parents began to talk about their little boy, laughing quietly so they wouldn't wake him.

The next morning, Bill finished his gravy and biscuits and tried to imitate his Dad, saying, "That was good. I'm going to school now. I'll see you tonight." His Mom just smiled. Her little boy thought he was all grown up now. As he reached the door she called out, "Stop it right there, young man. Give me a hug. I'll be here by myself all day long."

Concerned, he whirled around to look at her intently, "Momma, are you going to be okay? Why don't you go stay with Mamaw?"

She realized she'd worried him and said, "That's a good idea. Now you scoot off to school."

She poured her coffee and stood on the porch watching him walk to McGill's. She'd just finished her coffee when she saw him reach the gas pumps. She smiled, As she saw him searching the group for the girl who had talked to him yesterday. As soon as he found her, Bill stomped up demanding, "What is our bus driver's name?"

"It's Woodrow Thomas. He lives across the highway from Frank Wright's farm," she replied.

His response was cut short as the bus pulled up.

Chapter 2

After a couple of weeks, it became apparent to Bill's mom that school was just routine for him. Now he'd just go outside and play once he got home without first relaying any stories or problems.

Right before Thanksgiving, he came bursting through the door, "Miss Laura tied up Freddy Long today!"

Shocked, his mom turned and asked him, "What on earth are you talking about?"

"Freddy keeps getting up and playing with the stuff in the back of the room while Miss Laura is trying to teach. She paddled him a few times, but he just kept doing it. When he got up today, she made him sit back down and she tied him right there in that chair with a rope! She wouldn't even untie him for recess."

It was all she could do not to burst out laughing as his eyes were as wide as she'd ever seen them. She didn't know what to think about what had actually happened, so she questioned him further, "Well, what did he do then?"

"He cried when all of us other kids went outside to play.

But Miss Laura didn't untie him until it was time for lunch."

"Did she tie him up again after he ate?" asked his mom.

"No, she asked him if he was going to stay in his seat or did she need to do it again," he responded. "But that Freddy just said he'd stay in his seat no matter what if she didn't do it again!"

His mom asked, "Well, did he do what he said?"

"Yes ma'am. That Miss Laura can be really mean if you don't listen to her," Bill said in a hushed voice.

"Are you being a good student?"

"Yes ma'am. I promise. I really am being good," he swore.

"Well let's just keep this as a little secret from your Daddy. We don't want to upset him. I'm not sure how he'd like what happened," his mother cautioned.

Bill grinned, "Yeah, he might get real mad."

The first week of December Bill was so excited when he burst through the front door he couldn't even talk.

His mom raised an eyebrow and said, "Bill! Take a breath. Did Freddy get tied up again?"

"No, Momma. He sits in his chair all day long now. Miss Laura told us today we're drawing names for a Christmas party we're having in two weeks.

She said we'd need to buy a gift for the person we got. Ain't that great, Momma? I'll get a present."

She smiled, "And you know that means you'll need to get a gift for the person you draw."

His eyes got wide, "Aww, Momma. What am I going to do? I don't know how to do that."

"Let's see whose name you get and then we'll decide," she said calmly.

"Okay, Momma."

The next week was the longest of his short life. That Friday evening his Mom sat on the front porch watching for him. When he got to the barn, she could tell by his slow walk that her little man was upset.

As he started up the steps to the porch, she asked, "What's wrong? Didn't you draw names today?"

"Um huh." He said in disgust.

She hid her smile and said, "Well then, what's the problem?"

He shook his head and frowned, "I got an old girl's name."

"That's okay, son. Who is it?"

"Linda Kovsky."

"Kovsky? I think your Daddy works with her Daddy at the plant."

"Momma, you just don't understand. I don't know nothing about no girl's stuff," he complained. She could tell he was worried he'd not be getting his gift if he didn't come up with a solution. She took pity on him and said, "Momma will help you."

Saturday as they walked into Blue Ridge Pharmacy, she looked at Bill with a wink and said, "Okay, little man. Here's a tip. All girls like candy."

She watched as he walked over and perused every single box until he latched onto the box of chocolate covered cherries. He looked over his shoulder at her with a questioning gaze. She nodded and said, "That one's perfect."

The last day of school before the Christmas break, Bill took the package with him as he headed to the bus. She was anxious all day waiting to see how it went.

That afternoon he came running into the house breathless with excitement, "Momma! Look. I got a box of chocolate covered cherries, too!"

She grinned, "And did a girl draw your name?"

"Yep, it was Mary O'Neil. She's pretty nice."

Chapter 3

In early spring, Bill saw someone walking up the trail from the barn singing.

My Momma told me.
If I would be goodie.
She would buy me a rubber dolly.
So don't you tell her I'm your feller?
Are she won't buy me a rubber dolly!

As he got closer, Bill ran inside yelling to his mother, "Momma, there's a soldier coming to see us!"

She walked to the door and said, "That's your Uncle Max. He was drafted in the Army right after Christmas."

Bill ran outside to meet him. Max grinned at the child's excitement, saying, "Boy, have you really grown."

"I'm seven years old now," Bill said proudly.

"Congratulations. What'd you get for your birthday?" Max asked.

Shrugging, Bill said, "Nothin."

"What grade are you in?"

"I'll be in the second grade next year," Bill announced proudly.

"Do you like school?" Max asked.

"Yep. Do you like your job? Is it okay? Do you get to march a lot?"

"Oh yeah, a lot more than I want to," Max laughed.

"Do you shoot rifles? I bet being a soldier would be the best job in the whole world."

"It's good, but I'm not sure it's the best," Max said laughing as they approached the porch.

Bill's Momma hugged her brother-in-law, saying, "It looks like the Army's been good to you."

"Well, the food sure is good," he agreed, looking down at his belly.

"How long are you going to be home?" she asked.

"I'm on a ten day leave and then I'm headed for more training."

"Do you have any idea how much longer you'll be at Ft. Jackson?" she asked.

"No Roxanne, and that leads me to why I'm here. I have a problem because Old Red has discovered Momma's chickens. That old red bone hound sure does have a taste for them now. I was hoping my little man, Bill, could take care of him until I get back home."

Bill screamed in excitement, "Oh Momma! I'll take such good care of him."

"Taking care of a dog is a big job," she said sternly. "He'll need to be watered and fed."

Max said, "And you'll need to take him into the woods and let him hunt. He's a hunting dog. In fact, he's the best squirrel dog around these parts."

"Max, why don't you eat supper with us? Charlie will be home in a few minutes and that way you can talk to him about your dog," Roxanne suggested.

"I like that idea," he nodded in agreement.

When Charlie came through the door, Max shouted, "It's about time you got home, big brother."

"Is that your dog tied to my post? What are you up to?" Charlie said frowning.

"Can't pull anything on you, can I? I was thinking Bill could watch him while I'm in the army."

Charlie looked over at Bill, who was quivering in excitement. "I guess so, but Bill, that dog never comes inside this house. Understood?"

Bill eagerly agreed, "He won't! I promise."

His dad explained, "It's a lot of work taking care of an animal. Don't you dare come complaining to your Momma or to me when you figure that out, you hear?"

Bill looked down at the floor, "Yes, Daddy."

Max extended his hand to Bill, saying, "Is it a deal?"

Nodding, Bill said, "Oh yes, sir." Then he took off running towards the door.

His Mom yelled, "Come eat first!"

"Momma, I'm not hungry," he said as the door slammed. The adults just looked at each other and laughed.

Later as Max left he promised to bring the dog's house and some wire to make a pen for him on Saturday. He was true to his word that morning and he arrived just after 8 a.m. The Carpenters were still having breakfast when he walked in the door.

Roxanne invited him to join them and he grinned and said, "I'll take one of your biscuits and maybe one of those sausages to put in the middle."

She laughed, "Max, sit down and eat. I'll pour you some coffee."

Charlie looked over at his brother. "What did Momma think of Red's arrangement?"

"She didn't say anything. Now, Daddy told me to tell you when you and Red kill some squirrels, he wanted the brains."

Charlie shook his head, "Max, have you ever tasted squirrel brains?"

"Nah, have you?"

"Nope, but Daddy loves them. I have no idea why," Charlie said.

"Daddy eats possum. If he'll eat them, he'll eat anything whether it tastes good or not."

Roxanne had listened long enough, "You two sound like school kids."

Embarrassed, Max changed the subject. "Here's my address in case Bill wants to let me know how Red's doing."

She looked at the address and asked, "What's this APO and number?"

"APO stands for Army Post Office. The number is the location of that unit. If it moves, it still keeps the same number. If a soldier moves, he gets the number of his new unit. That's how they keep track of us," he explained

"That's pretty smart," she said.

Chapter 4

Bill had finally reached the end of his first year of school. When he got off the bus, he ran all the way home. Immediately, he noticed his mom working in the garden. It looked like his dad had just plowed it. As he ran down the middle of the row, she yelled, "Stop right there, young man. Take off those good shoes. They'll last you at least another year. You don't need to wear them in the summer anyway. I went barefoot my entire childhood, and if it was good enough for me, it won't hurt you one little bit."

He sat down and eagerly removed those dreadful, old shoes. He loved going barefoot. Now he and Red could wade in the branch anytime they wanted.

After a few weeks, he learned one of the pitfalls of going barefoot on a farm – the painful surprise of a **stone bruise.** He'd been chasing Red down the hill towards the barn when it happened. He felt a sharp pain near his heel and it stopped him in his tracks. He was afraid to look down to see how badly he'd hurt his foot and immediately wondered how on earth he'd tell his Momma.

When he tried to walk, he realized the only way he could was to put his weight on his toe because when he put down his heel, he could barely tolerate the pain. He hobbled back towards the house with Red running circles around him, wanting to play. About that time, his mom came out to check on his whereabouts and noticed him limping. She knew immediately he had a stone bruise and figured the best way to handled it was to ignore the problem. Bill came in trying to hide his limp and sat down at the table waiting for his dad to come in from work. Roxanne slipped outside to meet Charlie as he got out of his truck. He looked at her puzzled and asked, "What's wrong?"

She grinned, "Your little man just got his first stone bruise. I pretended not to notice. Figured you'd be the one to handle this."

He grinned back at her, "You decided that, did you? Okay, what do you want me to do?"

"I don't know. He'll be limping for more than a week. What did your Daddy tell you?"

"Oh my, you wouldn't believe it if I told you," he said shaking his head and heading towards the back porch.

She said, "Just tell him what he told you."

As Charlie sat down at the table, he winked at his wife. "Bill, your hands are filthy. Did you wash up?"

Without thinking, Bill jumped up and headed to the dishpan almost falling in the floor with his first step.

Charlie innocently asked, "What'd you do to your foot, son?"

"I wasn't doing anything wrong, Daddy. Honest."

"I know that, son. Looks like you've got what they call a stone bruise. It's going to hurt for a few days but I'm going to tell you what my Daddy told me when I got my first one. He looked at me and said, '**Son, walk it off**.' I know that sounds harsh; but believe me, it's the truth."

Bill jumped out of bed the next morning eager for the day, but as his foot hit the floor he remembered his stone bruise and groaned in pain.

Before he realized it, he felt tears slipping down his cheeks. He immediately stopped himself as he would never want his momma to know he'd cried over something so stupid. He remembered his dad's advice, walk it off. He took a deep breath and hobbled to the breakfast table. His mom had to fight her own tears when she saw her little boy being so brave. She knew she couldn't say a word, but she could see he was struggling. "Eat breakfast while I go to the mailbox," she said. Once she returned, she smiled and said, "Bill, you got a letter from Max." She opened it for him and began to read aloud.

Dear Bill,

How are you and Red getting along? Today we marched to the rifle range. It was about five miles from my barracks. They look just like the ones they have at your school. The only difference is this one's two stories high and has a latrine and shower. In a couple of weeks training will be over and I'll be getting orders telling me where I'll be going. I'll let you know when I do. Keep Red busy.

Your uncle,

Max

Bill was quiet for a moment and then asked, "Momma, what's a latrine?"

"Son, it's an outhouse."

"Oh. One day I'm going to be a soldier, Momma."

After a couple of weeks, Bill had completely recovered. By the end of the summer the soles of his feet were like shoe leather and could withstand even the most aggressive rock. He was dreading the reality of having to put shoes back on soon when school began.

Chapter 5

The day after Labor Day Bill walked down the halls of the old white school house in Epworth. He glanced over at his old classroom with all the kids as he kept moving towards his new second-grade classroom.

2nd grade Epworth Ga. Sept 1950.

He looked around and saw many familiar faces from the first grade. He moved to the seat located in the same spot he'd had in the class.

It didn't take him long to realize he was bored with the second grade. He sat impatiently waiting for recess.

When the bell rang, everyone jumped to their feet except the boy next to him. Bill was curious about him as he remembered him as being quiet and shy during the first grade.

He looked around and realized they were the only two left in the room. When the boy stood and tried to walk, Bill knew exactly what was wrong. He blurted out, "Do you have a stone bruise?"

Groaning, the young boy said, "I don't know. All I know is it hurts like the devil around my heel."

Bill looked at him in sympathy, "Well, how long have you had it?"

"A couple of days. I've been trying not to walk on it."

Bill smiled, "I had one of those last summer. My Daddy told me to 'walk it off.'"

The boy laughed, "That's exactly what my Papaw told me to do!"

Bill asked, "What about your Daddy?"

"He's in the army. I think he's someplace overseas."

Bill suggested, "Why don't you take off your shoes? You might be able to walk better. My name's Bill. What's yours?"

"I'm Tommy. I'm not sure Miss Birdsong will like me going without shoes."

Once outside, Miss Birdsong asked, "How's your foot, Tommy? Feel better without shoes?"

"Yes, ma'am."

She just smiled. "I had a few stone bruises when I was a young girl on the farm. This your first one? Do you know what the cure is?"

Bill and Tommy answered in unison, "Walk it off."

All three laughed. Bill decided he was going to like his new teacher. She reminded him of Mamaw Carpenter. She always knew exactly what to do and say. On the bus ride home he thought about his day and he couldn't wait to tell his Momma he had a best friend and that his best friend had a stone bruise.

He quickly adjusted to the routine of the new school year. His routine was about to change and he didn't even know it. The first week in November his Momma gave him a little brother named Roy. It was a huge change and he wasn't the center of attention anymore.

Every time Bill came home from school, he knew he'd find his Momma taking down diapers from the clothesline. Today wasn't any different. When she saw him, she asked if he could take the milk up to his grandparents, he jumped at the chance.

"Great, but Bill don't take Red with you. Remember Uncle Max said he really liked your Mamaw's chickens."

Bill grinned and headed to the house to get the milk. She yelled out, "One more thing, young man. You get home before dark!"

As he walked into his Mamaw's kitchen, she smiled and said, "You're just in time. I just used the last of the milk I had. You had supper yet, boy?"

"No, ma'am."

"Go out on the porch and tell your Papaw it's suppertime," she instructed.

He loved to eat at his Mamaw's house. She always had an apple pie for him or some other dessert.

Papaw sat down at the table and looked over at Bill, "You and Red found any squirrels yet?"

"No, sir. Daddy said he was just too busy right now."

Mamaw shook her head in sympathy, "That new baby makes it hard on everyone for a while."

The rest of the school year Bill would carry milk up to his grandparents three times a week. He would also enjoy her fine cooking.

Roxanne always answered Max's letters giving him an update on the family.

The last one they received said he'd finished basic training and would be stationed at Ft. Jackson for the next six months. She had told Max about the new baby and how Bill was suffering from a "lack of attention" lately. Shortly after that, Max had asked for his shirt and pants sizes, saying he wanted to reward Bill for taking care of Red. A few weeks later a package came in the mail addressed to Bill. It was Christmas in August for the Carpenter family. When Bill opened it, he found a brand new pair of fatigue pants, a shirt with US Army on the left side and his name on the right, an army belt and a patch on his left shoulder. There was also a matching fatigue cap that was too big for him now, but when Bill tried it on his entire face lit up, "It's too big right now, but I'll grow into it, Momma."

When he insisted on wearing it to school, his Daddy adamantly refused, reminding him he would hurt the other boys' feelings and they would think he was bragging. "You should only wear it in the field. Wear it when you take Red hunting."

Bill looked up at him with an extremely serious expression, "Like a real soldier?"

Charlie winked at Roxanne, "That's right."

She quickly moved to the kitchen so no one would notice how touched she was at Max's thoughtfulness.

Chapter 6

A couple of years had passed and Tommy and Bill had become inseparable. Once Bill had discovered Tommy's Daddy was a Captain in the army, he couldn't get enough information. Tommy had been born at Ft. Sill, Oklahoma where they had a lot of the barracks buildings their school was now using for classrooms. The ones Tommy had seen had been used as living quarters for the soldiers. As spring approached, the two boys would do their best to sneak a peek inside during every recess. Bill couldn't wait to get inside of one of the classrooms in this building.

A month before school ended for the year Tommy told Bill, "Daddy is coming home from Korea."

Excited Bill said, "I bet he will have some great stories."

A few weeks later, Tommy said, "When Daddy got orders for overseas, me and Mom decided to come here and stay with Mamaw Colwell rather than live out in Oklahoma. Now that he's coming home, we're going to go with him wherever he goes next."

The next morning Tommy told Bill, "Mom got a letter last night saying he'd be going to Ft. Hood, Texas. He has to be there by July 1st."

It was a blow to the gut for Bill. When he told his Momma, he broke down and cried.

She did her best to make him feel better, but she just didn't have the right words. Bill was inconsolable.

Later that evening, she told Charlie what had happened. "Sweetie, try to go easy on him."

Charlie just nodded. "I know how he feels. Losing a best friend is hard. Our little man is growing up."

Friday after work he surprised Bill with a new fishing rod. "Trout season just opened and guess what? I know a special place near Curtis Switch that always has fish biting. We'll leave early in the morning. That way we will have the best chance of catching enough trout for supper."

Roxanne got up and went into the kitchen. She was so touched to see Charlie treating Bill with such compassion. He'd had a hard life and didn't often show any tenderness to his son.

After supper, they went out on the back porch. Charlie said, "Son, go out to the smokehouse and get the mattock."

Once Bill returned, they moved to the back of the house where his Momma threw her dishwater. Charlie took the lid off of one of Roxanne's empty jelly jars. "Son, pick up the red worms as I dig them up." In no time the jar was half full. He put in some loose dirt and cut holes in the lid.

The next morning the men ate breakfast as fast as they could.

It was a twenty minute drive to the old metal bridge at Curtis Switch. As they passed the tracks, Charlie parked in an open space on the side of the road. He pointed at the river and said to Bill, "Looks like they've released water from the Dam. See how high the water is on the bank?" They grabbed their gear and walked west along the railroad tracks. Bill was skipping with excitement. This was all new to him and he had no idea what to expect. About fifty yards down the tracks, the river sloped a lot closer. Charlie pointed to a large tree on the bank and said, "That's our fishing hole. See how the water has cut under the bank? Let's go get us some fish."

Bill had never seen his Daddy so focused on something that wasn't work. Charlie showed Bill how to bait his hook and then he threw his own bait up river and let it drift down under the bank. As soon as it was out of sight, he yelled, "I've got one!"

In less than an hour, they had six trout. Bill had caught one and Charlie had caught the others. He smiled at Bill, "Let's clean these guys and get them home so your Momma can cook them up for supper."

When they got home, Bill couldn't stop talking. Roxanne smiled and hugged her husband. She whispered, "Sweetie, you did Good."

One night after supper his Daddy began to cough up blood. Bill could hear his mother insisting the next morning he go straight to the company hospital. Luck was with him and Doctor Hyde was there to treat him.

When he got home Roxanne wouldn't leave him alone until he told her what the doctor said. Bill tiptoed to where he could hear them. His Daddy stammered a little, and said, "Doc Hyde looked me straight in the eye and said, 'Charlie, there's nothing I can do for you. What you need to do is stop smoking.

If you don't, you're going to die pretty quick. I don't like my patients to die on me, so if you won't quit, don't come back to see me. Now get back to work.'"

Roxanne was surprised, "He really said that? What are you going to do?"

Charlie took his two cartons of Camels and put them into the hot coals of the kitchen stove. Then he placed a large red can of Prince Albert pipe tobacco in the center of their fireplace mantel. He looked at his wife, and swore, "I promise I will never smoke again. My promise to you and that Prince Albert Can will remind me to never smoke again and I hope it will teach the two boys to never start."

"Why don't you tell them that at the supper table tonight?"

He grinned, "I can do that."

For years Bill would see his Daddy take out a packet of peanuts every once in a while and place three or four peanuts in his mouth, but Bill never saw him smoke again.

Chapter 7

The day after Labor Day Bill was back in school for the fifth grade. This time he was in the barracks classroom – finally. Mr. Thomas, the bus driver, was always first in the morning dropping off his students. Bill only saw four people from the bus in his class. He studied the room. He wasn't seeing it as it was, but tried to see it as it would be if soldiers lived there. There was a large pot-bellied stove in the back of the room. He wondered who'd be responsible for building the fire. Suddenly the noise level was increasing and when he looked around, it appeared the class was now full and about to start. It didn't take them long to get back into the routine as they all settled in.

It was a cold, windy day just before Thanksgiving. The children ran across an open field in their rush to get to the classroom. When the door opened, they saw a rosy glow from the pot-bellied stove and Bill noticed the coal bucket appeared to be empty. He and the other four students huddled around the warmth of the stove. They'd only been there about ten minutes when someone opened the door to the classroom and yelled, "Fire! Get out of the classroom. Now!"

Bill quickly looked around and realized the only people in the room were he and his friends. There wasn't a teacher in sight. All four of them took off willy-nilly to rush for the door to exit the classroom. Some of the other teachers appeared to be lining up students in the field about fifty feet away from the building. Even though it was cold, every student was mesmerized watching the fire and didn't seem to feel the cold. As they watched, the fire began to consume other classrooms. The entire barracks building had burned to the ground before lunchtime and well before the local fire department showed up.

After lunch Bill's teacher walked the class across the ball field to the Methodist Church, located next to Vestal's Store. That was to be their temporary classroom. It was a huge adventure for the students and not a lot of learning was happening during the transition. The next classroom was the high school's chemistry lab located on the south end of the gymnasium. They remained in that location through the end of his 5th school year.

By the next school year, the county had converted the high school's auditorium into classroom space. This was the first time Bill had a male teacher, Mr. Griggs.

His style was completely different from the previous teachers Bill had. Mr. Griggs had a large, handmade half-inch thick paddle on his desk in plain sight of the wide-eyed students. While teaching, he would sometimes pick up the paddle and tap his palm with it. This visual worked. Not once during the entire year did Mr. Griggs have to use that paddle. To show his appreciation he gave each student a splinter from the paddle as a keepsake.

Chapter 8

Bill loved watching his Mamma hoe the garden and he always tried to get Roy to watch, "Come on, Mamma's in the garden. Let's go watch her."

"No way, that's boring."

To Bill she was fascinating to watch. In no time at all she could go from one end of a bean row to the other, cutting down all the weeds and pulling fresh dirt around the young plants. Her finished row looked like a freshly painted portrait. Every year he watched her and his desire to learn how to do it just like she did increased. The summer he turned twelve, he asked, "Momma will you show me how to hoe our garden? It looks like it would be fun."

"It is! When you finish a row and look back on it, you feel the pride of accomplishing a goal."

"Momma, what's a goal?"

"That's something you want to get done or achieve. When you grow up, what do you want to do?"

He grinned, "That's easy. I'm going to be a soldier."

"That's a goal. A big goal. Hoeing a clean row of beans is a small goal, but you still feel good when you get it done. Go get a hoe out of the shed and you can work on the next row of beans."

Bill ran all the way there and back. Their garden had plenty of beans and corn to use for practice.

He was in Hog Heaven. But what he didn't know was after she taught him to perform to her satisfaction, hoeing the garden would become one of his chores. Bill knew what a chore was, but he didn't care because he loved to work in the garden.

The family headed to Mamaw Bullock's house on Sunday after church. Roy was so excited he couldn't stand it and took off running to the porch. He loved her and she always had a little surprise waiting for him – and all the cookies he could eat. Roxanne watched this little ritual take place and protested, "Momma, you're spoiling him."

Mrs. Bullock just laughed, "That's what grandmothers do. You'll find out soon enough!"

Bill headed towards the other side of the house when he heard a strange noise. He immediately saw his Uncle Herbert throwing something at a stake sticking up out of the ground. Herbert was only two year older than Bill, but had always seemed so much older. He'd been the one who taught Bill how to ride a bicycle and catch spring lizards. Bill asked, "What you doing?"

"I'm practicing for the horse shoe contest in Epworth on the fourth. I need a partner. You want to learn how to pitch?"

Bill was surprised, "Really? You want me to be your partner in a contest?"

"You better believe it," Herbert said. "It's a lot of old men pitching horse shoes. With a little practice, we should be able to whup them easily."

Bill accepted two shoes from his uncle and immediately let them loose towards the stake. He quickly discovered it was a lot harder than he'd thought. Herbert let him throw for a while and then once Bill got the hang of the motion, he started giving out instructions.

The first thing he showed him was how to hold it. Bill couldn't believe the difference that one thing made in his throw. After a while he actually got a ringer and he was hooked. Herbert gave him some old horse shoes to take home for practice and Bill used his every free moment afterwards doing just that. Every once in a while his Daddy would come out and throw with him. He couldn't believe his Daddy used to pitch them all the time. After supper one night, Charlie said, "Son, why don't you go get that box out of the floorboard of the truck?"

When Bill returned, Charlie opened the box and handed him brand new horse shoes. He suggested they practice with those and assured Bill he'd be even better than Herbert.

When the fourth of July finally arrived, Charlie, Roxanne, Roy, Bill and Herbert were on their way to the Epworth Celebration. Roxanne watched Bill and Charlie, trying to determine which was the most excited. Charlie was frantically giving Bill pointers and instructions the entire way. "Take a deep breath and relax, right before you pitch," he said.

She couldn't stand it anymore, "Sweetie, let those boys alone. They're nervous enough and don't need your help."

"Yes, boss," he said grudgingly.

At the ball field, Herbert signed in and checked to see if they could use their own horse shoes. He came running back, excited they'd said yes. "We start at 9 o'clock," he said. He pointed over next to the wood line and said, "That's where we'll pitch."

Charlie got himself a cup of coffee and Roxanne and Roy got a Coke. Both competitors were too nervous to drink anything. The family just sat on the old wooden bleachers waiting for the correct time. Bill and Herbert were paired with a couple of boys their age who had just decided to compete a couple of days before the fourth. They'd never practiced pitching together. Bill and Herbert had half of the twenty-one points required to win before their competitors even got their first point. After winning the first one, the second was much closer.

By the third contest, the boys were doing much better and the scores were close. When Bill threw the winning ringer, Roxanne yelled so loudly everyone in the crowd turned to see who was so excited. The last competition would determine the overall winner and it was touch and go all the way to the finish. Herbert had whispered to Bill just before the game began, "It looks like we've got us two old farm boys. Just relax and get as many ringers as you can."

It was a good plan; however, the farm boys had the same one and finished with a ringer. Bill and Herbert came in second. They were feeling sorry for themselves until Charlie put his arms around their shoulders and said, "I'm really proud of you boys. I was never that good."

Chapter 9

It was late in the fall as Charlie drove his truck to the northeast side of their property and parked it where an old north/south trail began. It could no longer be used by his truck. As he got out, he handed the axe to Roxanne and place the crossed cut saw on his shoulder. "Boys, see that trail? It once was a road from here to Copperhill."

Wide eyed Roy asked, "When was that Daddy?"

"Oh, I guess in the late 1800's."

They all took the trail almost 150 yards up a little hill to where the northwest/southeast trail crossed. Bill knew it well, "Momma, this is the tree I killed my first squirrel in. Ain't that right, Daddy?"

Charlie grinned, "That's the tree and those two dead red oaks are what we've come to cut for firewood this winter."

He dropped the saw and took the axe from Roxanne and cut a wedge in one of the oaks. When he finished,

Roxanne said, "Bill, grab the other end of the saw. Let's cut it down so your Daddy can trim the limb off."

Bill loved to use that crosscut saw with his Mother. They had a smooth rhythm, but his Daddy was different. Charlie rode the saw, which made it hard for Bill to pull the saw through the log. Bill guessed his Momma knew that because she always pointed out a limb or something that needed Daddy's axe when it came time for them to saw.

Around noon, Charlie handed Bill some money. "Take this and go to Willard McGill's store and get us some Cokes, some dime pies and as many moon pies as the rest of the money will get."

"Yes Daddy!" At that moment Bill felt like he'd grown from a baby to a working member of the family. He stuck the money in his pocket and began to run on the northwest trail to the grocery. It was more than a mile away, but nothing he couldn't do. In Bill's excitement, he forgot that his Daddy had built a four-strand barbed wire fence around all the wooded area. After he'd been on the trail for about two hundred yards, it began to go downhill for about three hundred yards.

His speed increased to the max. Halfway down the hill, Bill hit the fence. To him it seemed to stretch about two feet and then hurl him backwards onto the trail. The shock of it made him feel like he was in slow motion – Bill didn't realize what had happened until he hit the ground on his butt. Then he began to feel all of his wounds. The top strand of barbwire had hit him on his forehead, the second on his chest, the third on his stomach and the fourth on his legs. He wasn't sure how hurt he was. He made himself get up just to see if he could. When he realized he was okay, Bill crawled through the fence and began to run again. He kept thinking Daddy would tell him, "Walk it off!"

When he got to the store, Mr. McGill told Bill it looked like he'd crawled through a briar patch. Mrs. McGill cleaned him up and put some Mercurochrome on his wounds. Bill couldn't believe it. That hurt worse than hitting the fence. On the way back, the excitement was gone. He walked all the way to the fence and part of the way back to his family. They were so happy to see the Cokes and food, no one noticed his cuts.

Chapter 10

Charlie had the hay cut in his meadow during the early part of June. Max had just been discharged from the army and was finding civilian life boring. He volunteered to rake the new cut grass into long rows of hay. Saturday morning, Charlie, Max, Papaw and Bill began the long task of moving it from the field into three haystacks. They were on the north end of the meadow next to a huge June apple tree. Charlie saw Bill eyeing the tree. The first limb was about five feet off the ground and he could see exactly what Bill had planned. He quickly squashed the idea, "Son, that tree is too big to be climbing. I nearly fell out of it myself. Now I'm telling you to stay out of it. You hear me?"

"Yes, Daddy." Bill couldn't help but continue to look at the tree. He couldn't believe how many apples were on it and his mouth was watering. He could even see some were turning red.

Trying to divert Bill's attention, Charlie pulled the tractor up to one of the rows of hay. While it was still running, he had Bill take a seat and push in the brake with his right foot and the clutch with his left.

Charlie put it into low gear and told his son, "Take your right foot off the brake and slowly ease up on the clutch." As the tractor began to move, Charlie said, "Push in the clutch," and the tractor stopped. "We're going to be back there throwing hay on the trailer. When we get it all picked up, I need you to move the tractor ahead by about 25 feet. I'll tell you when to stop."

Today was Bill's first driving lesson and by the end of the summer he would be able to drive that tractor as well as any adult.

While they were busy Max filled his pitchfork with hay and began to sing.

My Momma told me.
If I would be goodie.
She would buy me a rubber dolly.
So don't you tell her I'm your feller?
Are she won't buy me a rubber dolly!

Papaw whispered to Charlie, "It's nice to hear Max sing his **happy song** again."

Charlie nodded, "I can't believe how long it's been. I feel bad now about teasing him about that stupid song when we were kids."

"If you think about it. He never stopped singing it. I notice he would sing it every time you were around." Papaw laughed.

"By dogged you right! I guess he's happy to be home now?" They began helping Max pitch hay on the trailer, once the trailer was loaded, Charlie directed Bill to get off and he drove it down to the haystacks.

Bill's job was to stand next to the center post and pack the hay down with his feet as they threw it in his direction. It was hard work, but he loved it. He'd never felt such a sense of accomplishment and he ended the day feeling pretty darn good about himself and what he'd done. He enjoyed it so much he would bug his Daddy all summer, "When are we cutting hay again, Daddy?"

Charlie would smile and say, "Soon, son. Just be patient. The weather has a lot to do with when hay is cut. A lot of good hay can be lost if cut during a rainy week."

So he turned his attention back to the apple tree. He and Red would run down and check on the apples a couple of times a week. He could see several bright red ones near the top, but knew his Daddy was serious about him not climbing that tree.

Sunday after church the last week of June, he and Red went down to check on the tree again. He was surprised to see his neighbor, Clara Jean Griggs, there checking it out. She was a few years older, but always very friendly with him. In fact, she had been so helpful on his very first day of school and he had never forgotten. When he complained the apples weren't falling yet, she looked at him and said, "Well, why don't you just climb up and get some of them?"

"Daddy won't let me. Says it's dangerous. Besides, I can't reach that first limb," he complained.

She grinned, "Let me show you how." Then she walked over to the ditch next to the dirt road and brought back a large stick of wood.

Bill asked, "What's that for?"

"It's a stick of pulpwood that fell off of a truck last year." She leaned it up against the apple tree and used it as a springboard to reach the first limb. Bill couldn't believe a girl could climb a tree like she did. In a few minutes, she was throwing apples down to him and smiling. She climbed down and complained, "There're not quite ripe yet. Maybe next week."

Bill said, "But that's July!"

As she left, she said, "I'll meet you next Sunday after church."

This girl was a mystery. Bill liked mysteries and now he had his first crush on a girl.

Once he got to the house, he walked straight into the kitchen and asked, "Momma, why do they call it a June apple tree when the apples don't get ripe until July? Why don't they call it a July tree?"

She grinned, "I don't know. Go ask your Daddy."

Overhearing the conversation as he read the newspaper, Charlie said, "I asked Momma the same question when I was your age. Know what she told me? She said it was because city folks named the apple trees."

Max walked up on the front porch as they were talking. For the rest of the afternoon, Bill pestered Max about being a soldier in the army.

Chapter 11

Before church Bill was surprised to see one of his neighbors wearing a Boy Scout's uniform. "Bobby, when did you get that uniform?"

"Last week. Daddy is assistant scout master for Troop 32 in Epworth," Bobby explained. "We meet every Tuesday night in the basement under the school cafeteria. You should join. It's lots of fun. We camp out and hike trails."

Charlie walked up and Bill asked, "Can I join the scouts, please?"

"Where and when do they meet?"

Bill repeated the information Bobby had given him. Charlie frowned and said, "Son, there's just no way I can get you there every week."

Bobby's Dad was listening to their conversation and volunteered, "Charlie, I can take him. I'm one of the assistant scout masters and have to go. It won't be any trouble for me to take Bill."

Bill pleaded, "Daddy, please. I promise I will do all my chores."

Charlie just nodded, "Well, if it's okay with your Momma, I don't see why not."

Bill took off running to confirm with his mother. "Can I join the scouts? Daddy said I could if it was okay with you."

"Where's your Daddy?" she asked.

In less than ten minutes, Bill was on his way to becoming a boy scout. Tuesday evening he met Bobby and his father at the church so they could drive to the meeting. Bill was impressed with how the troop was run. He felt like he was in the army. He was assigned to the Antler Platoon and found out there were ranks. The first one he had to earn was Tenderfoot. Then Second Class, First Class, Star, Life and the top rank was Eagle. His scout master was Mr. Galloway, the druggist in Epworth. He quickly learned the troop did something together every month, like hiking or camping. His first camp out was at Jack's River near Hell's Holler.

On Saturday they hiked to the Flat Top Mountain Fire Tower. Bill didn't have a tent, so he was paired with Don Queen. Bill loved it. Don's tent was an Indian teepee. This trip gave him the opportunity to accomplish several of the requirements for Tenderfoot. Bill's goal was to reach that rank before school let out for the summer. One boy in the troop got in trouble because he didn't go on the hike, but trout fished instead. Hiking was one of the requirements for Tenderfoot so the boy wouldn't be able to achieve that rank on schedule because he had missed his opportunity. Bill could see that had put the scout on the scoutmaster's "nasty" list.

Chapter 12

Charlie had a saw miller come in and cut the timber on the farm the summer before Bill's last year in grammar school. After they'd been there a while, Charlie and Bill walked over to see how they were doing. It was a fun walk for Bill. At one time his Daddy had his own saw mill; and in fact, had used it to cut the lumber for their house. Bill was only four then, so didn't remember much about that. As they walked, his Daddy reminisced about his mill and Bill was fascinated listening to him talk. Bill asked," Why did you sell it?"

Charlie thought for a minute. Finally, he began to answer. "One day while I was sharpening the saw, Max started up the engine. I was pulled into the belts that turned the saw. I had cuts all over and spent a long time in bed at home recovering. Your Mom insisted I sell it."

As he finished the story, they came up on some pine limbs -- tree tops, or as his Daddy called them, tree laps. His Daddy looked at the brush, "It would be a shame to let all of that good pulpwood rot. Bill, you should cut the laps up for pulpwood.

They're paying over six dollars per cord.

What do you think? The hard part's already done, the trees are on the ground."

His first thought was he could use the money to buy a Boy Scout shirt. Bill couldn't wait to get home, He went to his Papaw's house and borrowed his razor sharp axe and bow saw. The saw was bright red and to him seemed really big as he needed both hands to cut the logs.

Then he needed to find out what a cord was. When school started in the fall, he asked his teacher, he was surprised to learn she didn't know. Luckily, Joe Green, one of his classmate's father, made a living cutting wood and he knew the answer. He raised his hand and said a cord was four feet high, eight feet long and four feet deep. After that day everyone in class thought Joe was a genius. That evening Bill took the axe, bow saw and a measuring stick to the woods. He had the enthusiasm of a kid with a new toy at first, but after a week's worth of hard work, it began to wane. The easy logs began to be consumed and then he had to cut a lot of limbs to get to the pulpwood sticks. Needless to say, his production dropped dramatically.

After a couple of weeks of just trimming and cutting he decided to haul his precious wood home. He selected the field above the house to place it so it would be easy to load later. Hauling the wood was another adventure in itself.

His Daddy had bought an old army jeep a few years before to use on the farm and there was just one little problem with it – it didn't have any brakes. His Papaw was always telling him, "Son. You do what you have to do on a farm."

Bill found if he kept it in four wheel drive and the gear in low range, when he turned off the switch it would stop. He also found out it would stop quick and hard. If he wasn't holding onto to something, it would throw him against the windshield. Bill learned another way of having fun on the farm.

With the jeep, he could only carry about twenty sticks of pulpwood at a time. He learned it took between 400 and 500 of those things to make a cord. His Daddy's easy project was beginning to get even harder. The owner of the saw mill didn't help either. Every time Bill thought he was finished, they'd move the saw mill to a different location.

With each move, they'd cut the pines first and that meant a new work area for Bill. This went on for nearly six months. Then one day the saw mill guys stopped by the house to see his Daddy. It had been raining for more than a week, which made it too dangerous to work. His Daddy looked at Bill, "Why don't ask them if they could haul your pulpwood today."

Before Bill could ask, the owner said, "We can do that. But I need to charge you five dollars to cover the fuel."

Bill didn't have a clue if that was a good deal so he just agreed. "Sounds good to me."

With the help of the men, He had all of the wood loaded in less than an hour. When Bill started to get in the truck, he looked back for his Daddy, "You're not coming?"

"No, son this is your business. You don't need me."

Bill felt ten feet tall. The trip to the wood yard and the offloading flew by. He had six cords of wood and the price that day was $6.22. They paid him $37.32 and when he paid the sawmill owner his five dollars, Bill cleared $32.32. He was rich.

Chapter 13

Bill was really liking the scouts. He quickly memorized the oath and laws. Because of his camping trip, he earned his Tenderfoot Badge in record time. The next award, Second Class, was a little harder to achieve, but he was enjoying pursuing it. He wondered if Army requirements would be as rewarding to him when the time came. In the previous week's meeting, the Scout Master talked about Camp Rainey Mountain, a Boy Scout summer camp. The rifle and archery ranges had really gotten his attention. He went home and began pleading his case to attend. He decided he'd do all of his chores without prompting and look for anything he could do to impress them. He knew instinctively his Momma was the one he needed to target. He really needed her to take him to Mull's Department Store in Blue Ridge to purchase a Boy Scout shirt. He didn't think she'd complain because he'd earned enough money to buy it from selling pulp wood. He overheard his Momma bragging to his Mamaw that he had done all of the work himself. He'd never tell her, but he'd already decided he would never again agree to cut pulp wood.

He was going to be a soldier and no way could that be as hard as cutting pine limbs.

Bill was surprised at how easy it was to convince his parents to let him attend the camp. His Momma even surprised him with a Boy Scout shirt. When Roy saw it, he yelled, "I'm going to be one of those in two years when I'm old enough!" Everyone laughed at his announcement.

Bill had never been as apprehensive as he was about leaving for camp. He and three others rode with Bobby's Daddy, who had gone to the camp when he was a kid. He had told them how much fun it had been then and how there was so much more to do now. It only took less than two hours to arrive and they had all settled in before the evening meal. Bill was to sleep in a three-sided wooden shed with three other scouts. On his way back from eating chow, he realized he had a strange feeling. He didn't want to talk to anyone – he just wanted to be alone. He didn't like it and was the first to crawl into his bunk. No matter how hard he tried, he could not fall asleep. It was well after midnight before he realized what was wrong. He was homesick. Everything was strange and unfamiliar. He missed his parents, but mostly he missed listening to Roy talk about his day as he fell asleep.

He wondered if Max had been homesick when he'd been at Ft. Jackson. Someday he'd ask him.

The next morning he woke with the same nagging feeling. It continued until he was taken to the rifle range and met Army Sergeant Breedlove. As soon as Bill shared his desire to be a soldier, they became instant friends. By supper, Bill wasn't homesick anymore.

After summer camp, Bill was motivated to improve in rank and obtain as many merit badges as he could. His first was wood carving. At night he'd go through his handbook and choose which badge would be the easiest for him to earn next. By the end of the summer, he'd already earned six. He'd also earned Second Class and was well on his way towards First Class, which was much harder. Learning Morse-Code was more than he could handle. He put all his efforts towards the others first. When school started, he had a major setback. Mr. Galloway had accepted a job in Atlanta and quit being the Scoutmaster. His leaving had a major impact on the troop because no one else was qualified to take over. Bill lost interest quickly and by Thanksgiving he was no longer involved.

Chapter 14

By the beginning of his 7th grade, Fannin County had completed two high schools – East Fannin and West Fannin. They moved the Epworth High School students to West Fannin. Grades 6 through 8 were relocated to the former Epworth High School. These classrooms were positively fancy compared to what they'd had before.

The 7th and 8th grades were rewarding to Bill. The teachers seemed to use stories to teach a new subject rather than just lecturing like the ones he'd had before. Since he could easily remember the stories he began to actually absorb their lessons. For all three years in the old high school building he'd had the same students in his classes. Even so, he'd never made another close friend since Tommy had moved away.

One day in the eighth grade Steve Johnson was showing another classmate a picture of his older brother, who was in the marines. Bill was drawn into the conversation. Steve was telling the other boy he planned on being a marine one day himself. Bill blurted out, "Well, I'm going into the army."

Billy Mull and Eddie Bennett walked up to the group. From that day on, the four boys spent every recess playing some type of strategic military game. They became the *Warriors*. They loved to play war. They'd build armies on paper and fight the battles during recess.

Their games lasted all year long. They had so much fun doing it that soon some of the other classmates wanted to join in. As the group expanded, new roles were added. Of course, the initial four were the sergeants. They decided officers didn't do anything – sergeants blew up the stuff and killed the enemy, not officers. Then a boy named Al from Hells Holler joined the group and made a suggestion. He recommended they change their name to *Mountain Warriors*. The name stuck.

When one of them saw a war movie, he'd come in the next day and detail all the events he'd seen during recess. They'd laugh when the girls wanted to join. Everyone knew girls couldn't be soldiers. Soldiers get dirty – girls don't. When the *Mountain Warriors* grew up to be freshmen in high school, they began to lose contact. Billy and Eddie moved away and the rest had developed different interests as they no longer had classes together. Only Bill remembered he still wanted to be a *Mountain Warrior*.

Chapter 15

The week before Thanksgiving, Bill was putting Roy on the bus and he noticed Roy had been crying. "What's wrong?" he asked.

Roy looked down at the ground, muttering, "Nothing."

No one was allowed to talk on Mr. Thomas' school bus, so Bill couldn't continue to question his little brother. When the bus stopped, Roy darted home before Bill could catch him. That night at the supper table Bill watched Roy trying to figure out what had upset him so much. When their Daddy was almost finished eating, Roy asked, "Daddy, are we farmers?"

Charlie looked thoughtful for a moment and then explained, "Well son, we have a hundred acres, twenty cows, a pig and your mother milks every morning and every night. We cut hay every summer. We raise corn, peas and beans. Yes, I guess we are farmers. And what's more important, son, is I'm proud of it. Why do you ask? Are you talking about farmers at school?"

"Nah, I was just wondering," Roy said. Bill knew at that moment something about that question was what had bothered his brother, but he didn't pursue it. The next evening as soon as they got home, Bill overheard Roy ask his mom, "Momma, are we poor?"

"No more than anybody else around us. Why?"

"A girl in my class told me only poor farmers wear overalls. She asked me if I had any long pants. When I said no, she told me, 'See there. Told you.' Momma, can I get some long pants and a belt for Christmas?" he pleaded.

What Bill heard bothered him. He didn't have any long pants either. Self-consciously he began to wear his long brown coat hoping no one would notice he was wearing overalls.

Chapter 16

The summer before Bill started high school, Charlie bought a new gas-powered 16-inch wide lawn mower. His Daddy showed him how to fill it with gas, check the oil, and to start it. It didn't surprise Bill when that was the last time his Daddy had any contact with that mower.

Bill fell in love with this new machine. Their lawn was really small and he'd been cutting it with a sling blade. It took him all day to cut it with that blade, but with mower he could cut it in less than two hours. After that, each time he cut it, he would expand the size of the cut area. By the end of the summer, their lawn was almost three times as large.

He enjoyed working with it so much he took it up to his Mamaw's and cut her lawn, too. In the past he'd cut it with the sling blade but only twice a summer. Now he cut it every time it grew higher than two inches. Mamaw always rewarded him with her famous fried apple pies. Her pies were worth more than money and he cut hers more often than anyone else's.

Word got out quickly.

He never had to ask for money because they always told him what a good job he'd done and gave him what they could afford. One of his uncles would give him twenty cents. His neighbor, Nellie, would pay him a whole dollar!

He had to admit his uncle's yard never increased in size, but Nellie's got as large as he could make it. He'd trim under hedges, around the house, under porches, and anywhere grass would grow. This paid off in his next business venture.

The fall of his freshman year he began selling **Grits**, a weekly newspaper that had the headlines from papers nationwide. He started with fifteen papers. If he sold all fifteen, he would earn one dollar and half. He walked his route on Saturdays. Even though he learned to ride a bicycle when he was ten, he didn't have one. He decided he was on Santa's naughty list because he never found one under the Christmas tree.

One Saturday when he was making his rounds to his regular clients, he went to Nellie's house. She was on the back porch and went inside to get her money when she saw him. While waiting, he checked out her oldest daughter's bicycle.

She was the girl that could climb their June apple trees like a squirrel. When Nellie returned, she asked, "Can you ride a bicycle?

"Yes ma'am."

"How far do you walk on your route?"

"I go down to the end of Barnes Chapel Road and then back down Preacher Thomas' road to Route 2. I need to go that far to sell all my papers. It takes me all day."

"Bill, do you want to borrow Clara's bicycle?"

"Yes, ma'am. That would be wonderful. I promise to take really good care of it."

She smiled, "Just put it back in the barn when you're done."

With the bicycle, he could go farther and faster. He increased his number of papers to thirty two and thought he was going to be rich. After a couple of months of selling the new amount, the **GRITS** Company sent him an award: a beautiful gold clock.

That Christmas his friend James got a new bicycle. Bill thought he must have been a really good kid that year.

James asked, "Bill do you want to buy my old one?"

"How much do you want for it?"

"Three dollars."

"It's a deal."

Monday after school, Bill went home with James to pick up his bike. It was painted white and didn't have fenders, but to Bill it was beautiful and perfect. He rode the old dirt road home trying to dodge all the mud holes. He parked it in the front yard so everyone in his family could see it. When his Daddy got home, he came in and didn't say a word. He washed his face and hands and sat down at the supper table like he always did. Roy couldn't stand it any longer. "Daddy did you see Bill's new bicycle?"

Looking sternly at Bill he asked, "Where did you get it?"

"James got a new one and sold me his old one for three dollars."

His Daddy snapped, "That's too much. Tomorrow you take it back to James and get your money back. You don't need a bicycle."

Bill wasn't hungry anymore. He sat and watched the family eat. The next day he did what he'd been told to do.

From that day on it seemed he couldn't do anything right. He was too ashamed to ask Nellie for their bicycle as he'd bragged so much about the one he was going to buy from James. Now he was back to walking. On a good day he could only sell 20 papers. He finally had them only send him 15 papers. The first Saturday in December it began to rain and by noon, it had turned to ice. He was at the far end of his route. When he got home, he had never seen his Mom so upset with him. Monday he sent a note and what money he had telling the **GRITS** folks he quit.

Bill hoped his luck would change. **WRONG!** The first of the year he came home from school and saw Roy playing on the front porch with a little gold horse. He didn't think much about it until he saw his clock on the mantle was missing a horse. He could see Roy had broken it off at the base. He didn't know if he should cry, tell his Mom or tell his Daddy. He decide to go to the outhouse and cry. It was almost three weeks later before his Mother discovered the missing horse. When his Daddy looked at it he said, "Son it can't be fixed."

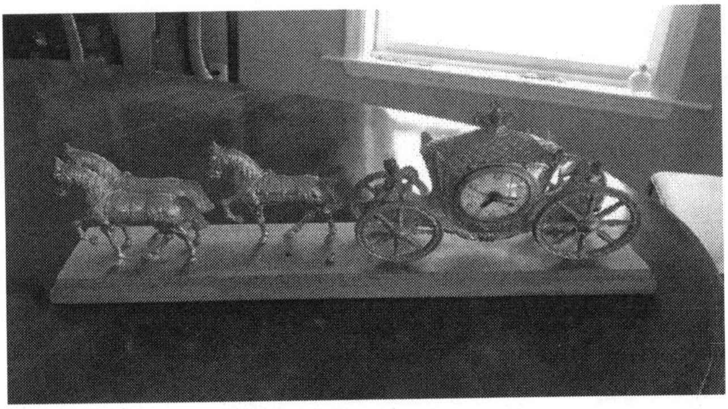

Chapter 17

The first day of freshman year Bill found himself the first person off the bus. When he entered the school, he noticed a lot of students were lined up in the hallway. Curious, he approached Joe Green, "Hey, why'd you get here so early?" He nodded towards the line and asked, "What's going on?"

"Daddy dropped me off on his way to work so I could get into the shop class. It always fills up first," Joe explained. Then he teased Bill, "Cut any more pulpwood lately?"

Grimacing, Bill stated, "No way! I'm never doing that again."

Joe laughed, "It's hard work, alright."

Bill blurted out, "Then why does your Daddy do it?"

"He says it's steady work and all he knows how to do. That's why I want to learn a trade," Joe explained. "I want to take shop and I want to join the FFA."

"What's FFA?" Bill asked.

"Future Farmers of American. This chapter gives each new member a ten week old piglet to raise."

Puzzled, Bill asked, "And what on earth do you do with that?"

"You have to show it at the county fair and breed it. When it has a litter you give one of them to the next new member."

Bill already had a pig at his house, so he said, "Maybe I'll join with you. That's easy enough."

Weeks later Bill had learned raising that pig wasn't uite as easy as he'd thought. Pigs are smart and stubborn. That stupid pig escaped her pen at least once a month and he'd come to despise Roy's smug voice yelling, "Bill! Betty Ann is out again."

Bill shook his head in disgust and took off running towards the woods in hot pursuit. He got her turned but she quickly darted into a small blackberry patch. Bill groaned, dreading how much those briars were going to hurt. He didn't hesitate and went right in after her.

When he cleared the last briar, he felt a sharp sting on his temple. As he crawled forward out of the blackberry bushes, he took off his green cap. He looked down in horror as it immediately turned bright yellow, and he realized that stupid pig had led him right into a yellow jacket's nest.

He panicked and stumbled to his feet as he looked down at his pants and saw they were completely covered in angry bees. He raked his hands down his legs killing more yellow jackets, as he ran towards the house quickly shedding his clothes. Every available inch of his uncovered skin had been stung. By the time he hit the back porch he'd escaped the yellow jackets, but he was only wearing his jockey shorts.

His shocked mother became hysterical when she noticed all the stings on his body as the nearest hospital was more than twenty miles away. Hearing the uproar, Charlie came out and took charge. He sprinted to the tool shed and returned with a hoe. Handing it to Bill, he pointed towards the lower part of his large garden. "Go hoe those last two rows of corn and make sure you cut every last weed before you quit."

Bill stood there in disbelief. Didn't his Daddy know he was dying? Did he hate him so much he wanted him to weed the garden before he passed? He whirled around and stomped to the garden feeling hurt and betrayed. Didn't his Momma love him either? Didn't they know he was hurting all over? By the time he reached the garden, Bill was furious.

He practically attacked that corn row, working at a furious rate. Moments later he began to sweat and as he did his pain began to dissipate. After thirty minutes he felt normal again and began to smile. His Daddy was really smart, but Bill still had to find that stupid pig.

Chapter 18

Since Bill was ten years old, his Daddy would take him squirrel hunting. Every fall Bill couldn't wait until 15 September, the first day of the season. Bill was always up before daylight each Saturday after the season began. He would wake his Daddy so they could go hunting together. It had been their ritual since Bill turned ten. A couple of years later Bill knocked on their bedroom door, whispering softly so he wouldn't wake his Mamma, "Daddy, it's time to go hunting."

He didn't respond as Bill expected, but instead he said, "Son, why don't you just go on by yourself?"

Stunned and excited, Bill whirled around and left before he had a chance to change his mind. After that Bill always invited him knowing he would give him the same response, "Just go on by yourself."

When Bill shared this little secret with his Mamaw, she smiled, "He telling you, 'I trust you, son.'"

After that Bill tried to be in the woods as often as he could. One day he came home with no squirrels, and his Daddy asked, "Did you see anything?"

With a big grin, he said, "No Daddy, but I killed two crows!"

"Where are they?"

"I left them in the woods. Why?"

"Don't you remember I told you we eat whatever you kill?"

"Yes Daddy, but they landed in the tree I was sitting under."

"Tell me son. How are you going to eat them if they are still in the woods?"

"Daddy, you can't eat crow."

"You should have thought of that before you killed them. What do you think I should do with you?"

"Daddy, I promise I won't do it again."

"Okay, let me make it clear what the rules are for you hunting. You eat whatever you kill. I will give you three rounds at a time. If you get a squirrel or a rabbit, I'll give you three more shells. If you waste them by shooting too fast or before you're within range, I won't give you anymore shells for the remainder of the season. Do you understand?"

"Yes, Daddy."

"You tell your Mamma you're going to be a soldier someday. Soldiers must always follow rules. Can you do that? Good. Wash up for supper."

Everything went well for Bill that year. However, the next year he got a little cocky. He thought he was such a good shot he kill running squirrels in brush. He missed not once, but three times. When his Daddy saw him with no squirrels, he asked, "See any? How many times did you shoot?"

"Three."

"You know the rules. If you want to hunt this year, you'll need to buy your own shells."

"Yes, Sir!"

If it hadn't been for Mr. Queen, who owned the little store next to West Fannin High School, Bill wouldn't have been able to hunt the rest of that year. Mr. Queen felt sorry for the boys and opened a box of shells and sold them individually. Mr. Queen sold them for eleven cents each for a .16 gauge shotgun shell. Bill never bought more than three shells at a time. When Bill was sixteen, he began hunting with Gerald, James and Gene.

Gerald had a friend who had a squirrel dog, which enabled them to hunt larger areas in a lot less time. After a few weeks, Bill was hooked.

He wanted his own dog. That was the main conversation when the three of them were together. One Sunday Gerald came running down the trail to Bill to deliver some fantastic news. One of his church members had a redbone hound who had puppies a couple of months before and wanted to get rid of them. All they had to do was go pick them up.

That turned out to be a bit of a problem, as it was fifteen miles away and they had no transportation. The puppies were near Galloway Road close to the river. It might have been fifteen miles by road, but by the way a crow flies it was just about five miles, which was more manageable. That meant they had to go straight through the woods and forge Sugar Creek in order to get there. Half a mile west on Galloway, they would need to turn up a narrow one-lane dirt road leading to the puppies' home. They took off at a pretty good pace and they got even faster the closer they got. As they went the dirt road, they could see an old man in a rocker on the porch. Bill said, "Boy he looks really old. He must be at least fifty."

"Yeah, I bet that's why he wants to get rid of those pups."

As they got to the edge of his yard, he hollered, "What are you boys up to?"

Gerald answered, "Mr. Green, we'd like to have two of your red-bone puppies."

He laughed, "You're too late. I've only got one left, and he's the runt. Do you still want him?"

They both answered in unison, "Yes sir!"

He pulled a half dollar from his pocket and said, "Tell you what I'll do. I'll flip this coin to see which one of you gets the dog."

Flipping it high over our heads he yelled, "Gerald, call it."

He answered, "Heads." The coin fell on the bare red clay and it was tails. Bill was the proud owner of a full-blooded red bone; and of course, he named him Red.

It was months until squirrel season started again, but that didn't stop Bill from taking Red to the woods. Bill was totally inexperienced when it came to training a squirrel dog. Gerald came up with a good solution.

He borrowed his friend's experienced dog and they'd take them to the woods almost every day over the summer. By fall, Red was ready and so was Bill. Bottom line was, Bill put squirrels in the freezer. For the four months of fall the Carpenter household had another ritual. Sunday breakfast was gravy and biscuits with fried squirrel. Bill would tell everyone no one in the world could make squirrel taste better than his Mamma.

Chapter 20

The next year at West Fannin, just before lunch one day in the spring, the principal came into Bill's classroom to get him. Raymond Weaver, a neighbor from across the mountain, was in his office as well. Mr. Dunn announced, "You boys are needed at home. There's a fire on your mountain and your families need your help. When the neighbor dropped them off, the fire department had just arrived with a bulldozer that had a large plow. It left a fresh track of dirt about four feet wide. The guy in charge yelled, "You boys follow along behind the dozer. Make sure no fire jumped across the freshly cut fire break."

The guy on the dozer cut a path to the top of the mountain. He had them come closer. "Boys, fire burns faster going uphill than it does going down. I'm going to turn down on the backside of the mountain just below the crest."

With the fire department, his family, Raymond's family and Mrs. Evans (who started the fire in the first place), the fire was out well before dark. It burned all of her woods, including her garden where it started. Mr. Weaver lost about half of his mountain and Bill's Daddy lost an area about the size of two football fields.

Bill thought the adventure was over, but that fall he found out differently. One evening his Daddy came home with several bundles of white pine seedlings. At the supper table he said, "Boys I need you both to plant these seedlings in the area that was burnt. You need to start at our property line and go to the fire break. Plant them six paces between the rows and the plants. Understand?"

"Yes sir," Bill asked, "When do you want us to start?"

"As soon as you finish eating."

After supper Charlie went to the truck and got a tool that had a T handle made out of steel welded to a large 3-inch-wide wedge.

He went to the edge of the yard and stuck the wedge in the ground.

With his foot, he pushed the wedge into the dirt and then pushed the handle forward about a foot and pulled it out. It made a perfect hole for the seedling. He dropped one into the hole and then placed the wedge about two inches behind the first hole and pushed it into the ground. Again he pushed the handle forward. The boys were amazed at how it closed the ground around the seedling perfectly. He then handed Bill the tool "Son, you plant one." He watched without saying a word and when Bill finished, he said, "Good job. Work until dark."

He then went in the house.

Being on top of that mountain with no vegetation to break the wind made it miserable. To them it seemed like the wind never stopped blowing and the closer it got to dark the colder it got.

With time Bill and Roy became a well-oiled machine. Bill would take six paces and shove the wedge into the ground and Roy would have a seedling ready to be planted. After a few days they could plant two and a half rows every evening. When they finished, they were both surprised and disappointed that their Daddy never even checked their work.

When Bill complained to his Mamaw, she asked, "Did you do a good job?"

"Yes, ma'am. Every row is straight and six feet apart; just like Daddy said."

"Son, your Daddy gave you the best gift a father can give his son. Are you proud of your work?"

"Yes, ma'am," he said looking at her in puzzlement.

"Well then you've learned the pride of achievement on a project. Think about it. You don't need your Daddy to tell you that you did a good job. For the rest of your life *the pride of achievement on each project* will make you happy and satisfied."

"Even if I become a soldier?"

"Especially then. When Max gets back, ask him how many times he achieved his mission?" she suggested, trying to make him see the value of his work. "The next time your Daddy does something hard on the farm, watch him and see how he smiles when he's done."

"Mamaw, I've seen him do that a lot."

She smiled down at him and winked, "Pride of achievement. Now come in the kitchen and I'll reward you for all that hard work with an apple pie. That okay with you?"

"Yes, ma'am. But you don't have to reward me."

She grabbed him up and hugged him tight, "See? It's already working!"

Chapter 21

One afternoon Bill, Jimmy, Gerald and James (Bill liked to call them *mountain warriors.*) decided to have a corncob fight around the three twenty-foot haystacks. They were excited at first but once the corn was removed from the cob, the cob was very light. This meant it lost momentum and distance very quickly. So the kill-zone was twenty feet or less. Even James, the youngest, could dodge an on-target cob.

The corncobs were just too light, so the next time they went to the corncrib to reload their arsenal, Bill realized there were plenty of leftover corncobs in the pigpen. The difference between the cobs in the pigpen and the ones in the crib was the ones in the pigpen were wet! That meant they were heavy, and heavy cobs would really fly. He couldn't believe he thought of it.

Fully loaded, they all moved back to their fighting positions. James was going to be Bill's first victim because he was predictable which made him an easy target.

Every time Bill threw a corncob that whizzed past him, he would stick his head out from behind the haystack and throw his cob.

Bill's plan was to lob a dry corncob underhanded with his left hand and then throw the wet one with his right. It worked. Just before the dry cob hit the ground, Bill hurled the wet cob as hard as he could at the place where James always stuck his head out. This time was no different; his head was exactly where Bill thought it would be. The cob hit James directly on the left temple, and he dropped like a rag doll. The other boys saw the blow and ran to James' side.

Jimmy anxiously whispered, "I think you killed him!"

Bill was in shock. To make matters worse, James' entire body began to twitch. It reminded him of a chicken with its head cut off. *How was he going to tell Daddy he killed James?*

Luckily, he never had to confess to corncob murder. James woke up. He didn't cry. All he said was, "Don't you go telling my mother!"

Bill tried to relax realizing how lucky he was that his parents would never know.

"Guys let's go play ball or something else." Bill suggested.

Jimmy grinned, "I know what we can do. Let's make horns out of Maple Bark like the Vikings."

James rubbed his head absently, "I don't know how."

"Don't worry, I'll show you how James." Bill volunteered.

Chapter 22

The students who lived in McCaysville were always taken home first on the bus. That meant the Gravely Gap students were stuck at West Fannin for an additional hour. As the year passed, several of them just decided to walk home if they lived within a couple of miles. Bill and a neighbor, Jimmy Edwards, who lived at the end of Thomas Road, were two of them.

The new Highway 5 was being constructed Bill's sophomore year. In the late fall, they were cutting a large opening just south of the school. One evening on the way home, Bill and Jimmy took a shortcut through the opening. As they walked along, they noticed wires coming up out of the ground. In front of that was a large truck sitting in the middle of the roadway. Bill hopped up on the running board, "Jimmy, there's a half full box of dynamite in here. Looks like there's a box of fuses, too! You get the fuses and I'll get the dynamite."

As soon as they jumped down on the ground with their spoils, they began to run as fast as they could to get away from the construction area. Jimmy asked, "Where are we going to put this stuff?"

"I don't know, but we sure can't put it near any of the houses," Bill said. They were looking for a hiding place all the way home. Just before they reached Bill's house, they noticed a couple of tree stumps had blown over. Both boxes fit perfectly under the roots. They looked at each other and smiled. Bill said, "Let's wait until Saturday to see what we can do with this stuff."

Jimmy asked, "What time?"

"How about 10 o'clock?"

"Sounds good, but I've got to get home." Jimmy took off at a dead run.

Bill had a problem come Saturday morning. Roy always wanted to do whatever Bill was doing. After fretting about the problem, he got an idea. He pulled out a jar of milk from the refrigerator and said, "I need to run this up to Mamaw." Then he turned to Roy and said, "You want to take it to her? You're old enough now."

Roy's eyes lit up, "Can I?"

As soon as the kid was out of sight, Bill took off for their hiding place.

Jimmy was already there, waiting impatiently. Bill showed him the flashlight battery he'd brought with him and Jimmy said, "Daddy always used a match to light the fuse. I'm not sure how to use a wire fuse."

Bill agreed, "Daddy does the same." He pulled one of the fuses out of the box and couldn't believe how long the wire was. "Wow! The wire over in the road is two feet out of the ground. Think how deep that dynamite is in that road."

Jimmy agreed, "That wire must be fifteen feet long. Where are we trying it first?"

"I don't know, but we need to get on the other side of our mountain," Bill warned. "Let's go down where the old grist mill was on Still House Creek."

"That's a great idea. It won't make hardly any noise down in that valley."

Bill pulled out one of the sticks of dynamite, "Daddy always cut it in half when he used it to blow up stumps."

Jimmy nodded, "It wouldn't make as much noise that way."

Bill cut the stick in half and put the other half back in the wooden box under the stump in their hiding place. The closer they got to the mill, the faster they walked. When they found the perfect spot, they realized they had a new problem. The wire was only fifteen feet long. That meant they'd be that close when they set it off. They looked around until they found a three foot deep ditch with a large oak on the side.

They decided they could hide behind the tree. Bill carefully put the fuse in the cut end of the dynamite and placed it behind a small tree. He laid a log on top of it. Jimmy strung out the fuse wire and hunkered down in the ditch. Bill joined him, pulling the flashlight battery out of his pocket. Squatting down, he slowly placed the fuse wire on the positive end of the battery. They were surprised when nothing happened. Jimmy asked, "Is that thing dead? Did you check it?"

"Yes. When I turned on the flashlight, it burned bright," Bill protested. After studying it for a few minutes, Bill said, "I know what's wrong! We need to put the wire on both ends of the battery, like in the flashlight."

Jimmy looked over at the fuse wire, "It's connected at the end."

"See if you can pull it apart," Bill suggested. With a little pull, it separated. They just looked at each other and laughed. This time Jimmy held the battery and Bill touched the wire to both ends. As soon as it touched, there was a loud explosion.

The impact knocked them both backwards onto the ground. They were laughing so hard. They'd forgotten to hunker down. Their ears hurt so badly they couldn't hear each other talk. Bill pointed at Jimmy and then back up the trail they'd used. He picked up the fuse wire and wrapped it around the stick like he did with his kite string. They walked much slower to their hiding place and by the time they had gotten there, the ringing in their ears had almost gone.

Bill said, "Next time we should tie this wire to the wire of the fuse and we'll be thirty feet away."

Jimmy said, "I like the way that sounds. I'm definitely going to be a lot farther away the next time we do this."

Bill pulled the same trick on Roy to get away the following week. When he met up with Jimmy, they decided to use two fuses this time. He pulled them out, along with one stick of dynamite from their hiding place. He looked over at Jimmy and said, "Think we should go to the same place or try something different?"

"Different. If we keep going to the same place, somebody might figure out what's happening and we'd get in trouble."

"Any ideas on where?" Bill asked.

All the way to Sugar Creek? I heard some men talking about how they used to dynamite the fish in Blue Ridge Lake. Let's try that on some of those deep holes on the creek."

Bill's eyes got huge, "What a great idea! Let's go."

All the way there, they kept taking turns suggesting which hole to try first. They finally chose two that were fairly close together. They really wanted to see if they could kill some fish, but also didn't want to get caught. They decided to try the deeper hole first since they only had thirty feet of wire and didn't want to make their ears ring this time.

When they got there, they were ready to connect the wires in less than five minutes. This time they laid down on the ground in a small ditch. When they touched off the dynamite, they didn't feel the impact at all.

They checked the creek and all they could see was a muddy hole. They moved on to the next one with forty-five feet of wire. This time they only heard the explosion and it produced two horny head fish, about eight inches long.

Bill said, "Why don't you take these home? I'm not sure I can explain how I came up with them today."

Jimmy just shrugged, "That's easy. I'll tell momma you gave them to me."

They laughed as they walked home. The adventure went on for a few more weeks and then one day Jimmy pulled Bill aside before they went into homeroom. He whispered, "Yesterday at church I heard some people talking about hearing dynamite going off on Saturday. One guy said he thought it was the highway crew, but found out they don't work on weekends. Our preacher told them to call the sheriff the next time they heard them. What should we do?"

Bill said, "I don't know. Let's quit while we're ahead. Make sure you don't go anywhere near those stumps."

The rest of the school year Bill would look over at the stumps on his way home to make sure nothing appeared to have changed. For a few Saturdays, Bill felt guilty about how he'd fooled his little brother to escape to go play with the dynamite. As soon as it was warm enough to take off their shoes, Bill asked Roy if he'd like to go with him up to Mamaw's. Roy was so excited he chattered the entire way. His conversation always centered on the large ditch below Mamaw's house. "How long has it been there? Did you play in the sand when you were eight? Where does all that water come from? Can we play in the sand today?"

Then he went silent. Bill looked over at him and grinned, "Daddy said it was there when he was a kid. I was ten the first time I played there. The water comes from Highway 5 when it rains." He stopped talking and looked at Roy, "And yes, we can play in it today. Just don't tell Momma."

Roy's eyes widened, "No way would I do that. She can get really mad sometimes."

After they dropped off the milk, they detoured to the sandy bottomed ditch. The game was to see how far you could jump off the bank into the deep sand. They had marks on the bank from their best attempts. Bill could jump three times farther than Roy. Roy didn't care about that – he just wanted to break his own personal record. Bill's first try was a little short of his best attempt. He decided to make a running start on the next try. It worked and he landed almost three feet beyond anything he'd achieved before. That was the good news. The bad news was he came down on a broken bottle and cut a gash about two inches long on the ball of his left foot. Bill hobbled up to Mamaw's back porch, calling out for her. She came out, concerned, asking, "What on earth have you done to yourself?"

As he explained, she sat him down on the edge of the porch and went inside. She returned with a wash pan of water, a clean white cloth and a needle and thread. She washed his foot gently, cautioning him, "Son, I need to sew this up quickly before the feeling comes back."

She began to sew it up just like she was hemming a dress. Bill sat there amazed. It didn't hurt at all. When she finished, she poured mercurochrome on the wound and tied the white cloth around his foot. "There you go. Just keep it clean and you'll be okay."

Bill's face turned pale contemplating the ramifications of his injury and begged, "Please don't tell Momma."

She hugged him and turning said, "It's our little secret, isn't it Roy?"

Roy nodded solemnly.

Bill was amazed that he could walk without pain. As soon as he got home, he sent Roy to get him his socks and shoes. For the next week he did his best not to walk in front of his parents. It worked; however, every time he made Roy mad, he threatened to tell momma about their adventure.

Late one night, Roy was pleading for him to tell him another story about ponies and Bill just wanted to go to sleep. Roy threatened him for the third time, "I'll tell Momma in the morning if you don't do it, you just wait and see." Bill was tired and disgusted, but made him an offer he couldn't refuse, "If you promise never to tell Momma about my cut foot, I'll show you some Doodlebugs."

Roy just glared at him suspiciously, 'Hah! I'm not stupid. There's no such thing as a Doodlebug, that's just what Papaw calls me when he wants me to do something."

"Honest, Papaw didn't make up that name. Tomorrow when you get home from school, I'll prove it to you."

Roy was hooked and asked hesitantly, "You promise?"

"I do," said Bill. "Now go to sleep."

After walking home with Jimmy, Bill made it his mission to locate the elusive insect. He remembered seeing some under the front porch of the house. When he checked, he was surprised at how many there were now. He sat patiently on the front step watching for Roy. He couldn't help but laugh at how hard the kid was running in order to get home. He got up and moved to the corner of the porch, waving at Roy to catch his attention. Roy was totally out of breath when he slid to a stop, "Show me. You promised!"

Bill took him under the house and pointed to the ground, "There they are."

Roy looked at the upside down funnels and then back at Bill, "That ain't no Doodlebug. They're just holes in the ground."

"Now listen. Get down as close as you can right over any one of those holes and sing, "*Doodlebug, Doodlebug, your house is on fire.* Then just watch the bottom of the funnel. When he hears you singing, he will start to move."

Roy did as directed and barked out in surprise, "Ohee! They're moving."

When it stopped moving, Bill encouraged him to sing again. After a few minutes, Bill used the spoon he had to lift out the bug. From that day forward, he never had to worry about Roy ratting him out to his parents.

Chapter 23

"What's got you so upset?" Roxanne asked when she heard Charlie muttering to himself.

"You won't believe me if I tell you. Daddy bought a mule. Why? He always made us boys do the plowing. He's too old to work a mule and he will get hurt or killed."

Roxanne laughed, "It's that all? Your Daddy has been retired more than a year. He's just bored. Don't say anything to him about that mule. All you'll do is make him mad."

Charlie grinned, "Yes, Boss."

Bill and Roy couldn't help overhearing their parents. Roy whispered to Bill, "Can we go see it after school tomorrow?"

"Yeah, but don't say anything to Momma. When we get off the bus tomorrow, we'll go to Papaw's first. That way she can't tell us no."

Roy nodded in agreement, "Yeah, you know she'd say no if we asked."

When their Papaw saw them coming up the trail, he got out of his rocker on the porch and met them half way. "Boys, come let me show you something in the barn."

There was excitement in the air. Roy said. "It's your mule I bet."

Papaw laughed, "You're right little Buddy. Have you ever ridden one?"

"No Sir. I ain't even touched one."

Papaw began to teach Bill how to harness the animal. When he finished, he picked up Roy and put him on the mule's back. Bill stood back and watched Roy grin from ear to ear. "Do you want to ride some, little Buddy?"

Roy was so excited he began to jump around on the mule's back, which scared the mule and caused him to buck. It made a couple jumps before Papaw pulled Roy off. Roy hugged Papaw's neck so hard it was difficult for him to breathe. "I've got you. You're okay!"

When Papaw sat Roy on the ground, he said, "I want to go home now."

Papaw told Bill, "Take her to the barn and hang the harness on the wooden pegs. Me and my little Buddy will wait out here."

It took Bill a while to figure it all out and by the time he got back to the shed, Papaw and Roy were on the porch eating fried apple pies.

As Bill approached, Papaw said, "We've had enough fun for the day and you boys better get home before your Momma tans your hide."

A couple of weeks later, school was out for the summer. Bill wasn't really surprised that Roy didn't want to go over to Papaw's with him and didn't push it. He had seen the fear on Roy face that day. Maybe later they could ride the mule together, but for now Bill used the excuse of taking Mamaw milk so he could go. Roxanna smiled at his actions. She remembered how he'd acted when he first started school. She liked that old mule, she brought back wonderful memories. She could pretend as well as the boys.

As soon as Bill had given the milk to his Mamaw, his Papaw said, "Let's go down to the barn. I got some new stuff to show you."

When they got to the barn, Papaw pulled out a couple old plows. Bill could see from the new wood and metal that he'd had to do a lot of repair work. "We can put old Maud to work with these. "Go catch Maud and I'll show you how to harness her."

Bill didn't say word. He grabbed her bridle and ran to the gate. He was surprised when Maud walked to meet him. Papaw put on the collar and harness. Bill watched every step intently. Papaw hooked her trace chains to the single tree on one of the plows and handed the reins to Bill, "Let's take her over to the bottom of Mamaw's garden and

Lay off some rows so she can plant corn and beans."

When they got to the garden, Papaw said, "Plow a row about three feet below those peas."

Bill did as he asked. As soon as they started, Maud picked up her pace and they zoomed across the garden. Papaw walked across the field and helped Bill turn her around. They both looked at the small ditch he'd just cut. Papaw asked, "What do you think?"

Bill couldn't believe how crooked it was. "Papaw, it's more like a snake's trail."

"What did you do wrong?"

"Papaw, I don't know. I thought I was plowing a straight line."

He smiled, "You didn't keep the plow level. When you leaned it to the left, the plow moved to the right. Leaned to the right, it will go to the left. On the way back, don't touch the reins and Maud will walk straight to where we have her pointed. Your job is to make sure the plow stays level all the way across."

Papaw smiled watching him concentrate on keeping the plow level.

When Bill got to the end and turned around he could see Papaw grinning. "Boy, I couldn't have done better if I tried."

"Papaw why didn't you tell me how to plow the row on the first row?"

He grinned, "Over the years I've worked with a lot of young boys. I learned they think they know how to do everything. Your Daddy was the worst. Don't get me wrong; he has some great qualities, but listening isn't one of them. You're your Daddy made over. Never forget that, and you have some big shoes to fill. When I let you plow that crooked row and you saw the results, you wanted to make it better. You listened! Then you followed my instructions to the letter. How do you feel?"

"I feel good. I'm proud of that row."

"You should be and I'm even prouder of you. Now can you plow two more rows just like that?'

"I can try."

Chapter 24

Roxanne took out two jars of milk from the refrigerator on Saturday morning and said, "Take these up to your Mamaw's and take Roy with you. You guys can spend all day with them. Your Daddy and I are going to town and won't be back until around 4 o'clock."

Bill agreed, "I'll watch him, Momma."

"I'm eight years old! I don't need anybody watching me," Roy protested.

Roxanne smiled. She vividly remembered Bill's first day of school and how he'd shown his independence. "Roy, he just meant he'd tell you when it was 4 o'clock"

Bill nodded and changed the subject, "Think Mamaw will have any apple pies on hand?"

Roy agreed quickly, "I bet she does. She knows how much I like 'em."

They both laughed at how quickly they'd been able to distract Roy from his hurt feelings.

As they walked up to the grand parents' house, Bill asked, "Do you know what Momma and Daddy are really doing? Have you heard them talking about anything?"

Roy thought about it for a minute and then said, "I ain't heard nothing."

"Are you sure you didn't hear Momma yelling at him for something?"

"She was mad he stayed late at the Sluder's house last Friday." Roy said.

"What was he over there for?"

"I don't know," Roy said absently. "He goes over there some Fridays."

Bill said, "I guess we can play in the sand pile some, but I'll be checking it for glass first."

At 4 o'clock they took off like a shot running all the way home. They arrived just as their parents were driving up. Charlie said, "Bill, help me carry this into the house."

"What is it Daddy?" Bill asked curiously.

"You'll see, son."

When he took it out of the box, Roy looked at it and said, "Daddy, what is that thing?"

Charlie grinned, "That, my son is a Television."

Everyone was totally quiet until he'd attached the antenna and plugged it in, quickly turning it on.

Bill was watching closely, but didn't see anything. Finally, he asked, "Is it broke?"

"No, son. It just needs to warm up like our old radio."

When it finally flickered on, there was so much snow on the screen they could barely make out it was a man. Then Charlie started moving the rabbit ears around until he managed to get a clearer picture. By that time, the boys had lost interest.

Charlie kept trying for days to get a better picture on his new television. The guys at work suggested aluminum foil wrapped around the rabbit ears, which improved the reception some, but the snow was still obvious.

One guy finally told him, "Charlie, put up an outside antenna and point it towards Chattanooga."

That sounded like it would work, but he was having a hard time justifying spending any more money on the project, but when Friday night came and he couldn't make out the fight, he knew exactly what he needed to do. He'd been watching them at the Sluder's house every week, but this week he stayed home to watch this particular fight on his own television. Unfortunately, he missed it. At breakfast the next morning, he told Roxanne, "Me and the boys are going to town. We'll be back as soon as we can."

She smiled, "Going to get an antenna, huh?"

"Yeah, looks like that's the only way I'm going to fix that blasted thing," he admitted grudgingly.

"Charlie! Watch your mouth in front of these boys."

Bill glanced over at Roy questioningly. He had no idea what his Momma was talking about. He and his friends said "blasted" all the time.

They were back before noon and had the antenna mounted on the eaves of the house less than two hours later.

Once the television warmed up, it was clear on two channels, but snowy on the other. All three boys were happy. The first show was a western, Gunsmoke. Roy was immediately addicted. He liked Lassie, and the Howdy-Doody Show with Buffalo Bob.

Howdy Doody Show, **Buffalo Bob**

Bill would secretly watch American Bandstand, but he didn't want any of his friends to know.

Dick Clark

Chapter 25

Going to his next class, Bill saw Jimmy standing at the entrance to where students board the bus. He was holding an apple, but when he saw Bill he pulled his knife from his pocket and cut it in half. "Here, take this half. I don't have time to eat the whole thing,"

"Thanks, buddy."

"Are you going to the football game tonight?" Jimmy asked.

"I really don't care all that much about football," Bill said.

"You've got to go. They've won a couple of games and need a crowd to cheer them on. Besides, there's going to be a sock hop in the gym after the game."

Bill looked puzzled, "What is a sock hop?"

"You've never been to one? It's a dance party. It's called a sock hop because they make you take your shoes off on the gym floor and you dance in your socks."

That got Bill's interest. "I'm headed to class. Let's walk home later today."

"Sounds good."

As they walked home, they agreed on a time to meet at the football stadium gate. It was an exciting game and they won, but Bill was more interested in finding out what a sock hop was all about. When they got to the gym, they paid the guy at the door and he directed them where to put their shoes. The boys walked across the court and moved up to the third row of the bleachers. Bill couldn't believe how busy it was. When the music started, the basketball court filled with students doing a strange dance. He asked, "What's that song? I've never heard anything like it."

Jimmy laughed, "That's *Willie and the Hand Jive.*"

The next song was a slow one and Bill was shocked when Jimmy stood and asked a girl to dance. When he finished, Jimmy came back and nudged Bill on the shoulder, "What are you waiting on? Why aren't you dancing?"

Bill was embarrassed, "I don't know how. How on earth did you learn?"

"At the teen canteen in Blue Ridge," Jimmy explained.

Bill didn't know anything about Blue Ridge or sock hops. He watched a couple more songs and when Jimmy started slow dancing with another girl, he slipped out and walked home.

On the way he thought about the situation and then remembered how Roy must have felt when that girl had made fun of him wearing overalls.

Bill had lots of questions for Jimmy the following week. "Where's the teen canteen in Blue Ridge? Do you have to pay to get in?"

Jimmy grinned, "It's on the south side of town near Kaye's Auto Parts."

"Oh, okay. But do you have to pay?" Bill asked impatiently.

"No, it's free. Only rule is if you leave, you can't come back in for the rest of the night."

"That's okay, but how do we get there?" Bill asked.

"I hitchhike," Jimmy said.

Bill could tell he was kind of embarrassed about it, but he couldn't help but continue with his questions.

"Is it hard to do?"

"Nah, why don't you meet me where Thomas Road meets the new Highway 5 on Saturday around 5 o'clock? If we meet then, we'll have time to get a Coke float at the Rexall Drug Store," Jimmy suggested.

Bill got excited. It was all new to him and the idea of hitchhiking even sounded a little dangerous. He certainly knew his parents probably wouldn't approve.

The first car that passed them after Jimmy stuck out his thumb stopped. Bill couldn't believe it was this easy. Jimmy grinned. It was his neighbor, but he didn't want to tell Bill and spoil the moment. When they climbed in the back, the driver asked, "Where are you boys headed?"

Jimmy said, "To the Rexall to get a Coke float."

"Boy, they are good, aren't they? You two are in luck as we're going to the movie right next door."

After the boys had their float, they walked down the street to the canteen. Bill didn't know what he'd expected, but he was surprised when he saw a single story, white building around fifty feet wide and hundred feet long. It looked like they were just opening the doors as they walked up and everyone was pushing their way inside. Jimmy led the way to the dance area while Bill stared at the little record player on the small stage. He watched two girls move to it and place a couple of records on it before returning to the metal chairs lined against the wall. The first record was a fast dance. Jimmy pointed to the chairs on the other side of the room and they headed that way to sit down. Bill was mesmerized watching the way the dancers were moving to the music. One couple really got his attention. He loved how easily they moved together. Jimmy was talking, but Bill wasn't listening. Jimmy shoved him on his shoulder, "Why don't you go give it a try?"

"Maybe later," Bill mumbled and continued to watch their every move.

The next song was a slow dance and Bill found yet another couple he liked to watch. Without realizing it, he began to move his feet a little. Jimmy laughed, "At least your feet want to dance," Bored, Jimmy stood and walked over to ask one of the girls to dance. Bill remained seated watching for almost an hour before asking one of the girls he'd been watching to dance with him.

When she quickly agreed, he apologized, "I'm not very good, but know you are. Will you teach me?"

She smiled widely, "I would love to. I'm Jenny. What's your name?"

"Bill."

"Well, Bill. Let's dance," she encouraged. She made it easy for him as she led and helped him learn the same steps her partner had done when he was watching them. He only did slow dancing that night. He had the bug. When the canteen closed, he and Jimmy walked across to the city limit sign on the new Highway 5. To Bill's surprise, the third car that came by took them all the way to McGill's Grocery.

That old saying, "Little Boys Have Big Ears" applied to Roy as he listened to Jimmy and Bill talk. He knew what a canteen was because he watched all those westerns with his dad, but he couldn't figure out what was different about a teen one. Finally he decided to just ask, "Momma, what is a teen canteen?"

"I'm not sure. Where'd you hear that?" she asked, puzzled.

"Bill and Jimmy talked about going there Saturday," he offered up proudly.

She just shook her head, "I'm sorry, but I have no idea. I will find out and when I do, I will let you know. But let's just keep this as our secret for now, okay?"

"Yes, Momma. I like secrets."

When Roxanne got to the grocery store Saturday morning, she had Charlie ask June Taylor if he knew anything about a teen canteen. June was more than willing to tell them what he knew. "It's where the teenagers go to dance. The VFW lets them use their building on Saturday nights.

That fine couple that work at the post office chaperone them. They have a record player and all the kids bring their records from home and play them.

It's free and they can stay all evening; but there's one iron clad rule – if they go outside, they can't go back inside that night. It's a great, safe place for them to have fun and a lot better than cruising their cars between the Tastee Freeze and Lance's all night. Where did you guys hear about it?"

Roxanne answered, "Our son, Bill, was wanting to go there tonight."

June said, "You should encourage him. He won't get into any trouble there."

As they drove home, the subject came up. Roxanne said, "Now I know why he's been watching that American Bandstand show every day until you get home."

Charlie was clueless, "What's an American Bandstand?"

"It's a show where teens do different dances to all the new records that come out. I really like some of them. Sometimes it's hard to pretend I'm not listening, so I just stay in the kitchen. Charlie, our boy is growing up."

"Are you okay with him going to dances?"

"Yes, I'm hoping it will help him get over being so bashful," she said. "He's your son. He reminds me of you when we first met. How long did it take you to get up the nerve to even speak to me?"

He muttered, "Ah, about a year."

"I remember trying to talk to you at church, but when you saw me headed your way, you'd scrunch into the middle of whatever friends you had close by," she laughed.

He grinned, "I was playing hard to get."

"Yeah and your boy is doing the same. Problem is no one is even looking at him he's so shy."

"Guess that means you're comfortable with letting him go," Charlie offered.

"Yes, I am, but we can't push him. Let's just not say anything and wait and see where it goes," she suggested wisely.

He was just fine with that, "Sounds like a plan. I wouldn't have any idea what to say anyway."

"You could come up with some responsibilities for him. It might help him feel like a man. You said that's what your Daddy did," she prompted. She really liked this time they had alone when they went to town. It gave them a chance to talk about all the issues with the boys without anyone overhearing.

They rode in silence for a few miles and Charlie blurted out, "I know what I can do. I'm not telling you, but I think you'll like it."

"Charlie Carpenter, you know I won't sleep a wink tonight!"

He grinned and said, "Sorry about that."

Chapter 26

Bill was feeding the animals on Sunday morning while Roxanne was milking. When he got to Betty Ann's pen, he was shocked to see his Daddy standing there. "Son, you've done a wonderful job on that pig. When I think about it, you've been a great help on the farm. Max and I taught you how to cut and store hay, your Papaw taught you how to plow, and your Momma's got you doing a great job in the garden. Now I need you to do me a favor. The only thing I see you're missing is you don't know how to milk a cow. The favor is for you to ask your Momma to teach you and then I'm asking you to help her with the milking. She works harder than anyone in our family, even me. I can't help her, but you can. Will you do that for me?"

Bill couldn't believe his Daddy had that much confidence in him. "Yes, Daddy. I'll ask her today after church."

"Great. Son, why don't you approach it like it was your idea. She doesn't need to know about this talk."

Bill nodded and grinned, "Understood. If she knew we talked, she might think you forced me. Daddy, I really do want to learn how and to help Momma."

Bill grabbed the 5 gallon slop bucket that contained the leftovers from the day's meals later that evening. He always gave it to Betty Ann as a special treat. He rushed to catch his Momma on the way to the barn. Instead of breaking off and going into the pig pen, he followed her inside the barn and watched her dig out some dairy feed for the cow. When she finished, he questioned her, "Momma, how much do you give her?"

"About a gallon. Why do you want to know?"

"I was thinking I might like to learn how to milk. Is it hard?" he asked, tentatively.

"It can be if it's not done right," she said. "Go empty that bucket and I'll show you."

He almost ran to the pen and dumped the entire contents of his bucket into her trough. When he returned, Roxanne was just sitting down on a little stool. "First you have to wash her tits so you don't dirty the milk," she said.

Bill had always wondered why she carried water in the milk bucket. Then she slowly showed him how to hold the tit, "Start at the top and squeeze it down." When she did, a stream of milk hit the bottom of the empty bucket startling Bill. "You keep doing this until she's dry. You always have to milk her until she's dry. That's very important. Do you want to try?"

"Can I?"

"Sure, sit down and be gentle," she cautioned.

It was a slow start for him and after about thirty minutes she took over. She laughed, "She'll be out of dairy feed at this pace. You can try again tomorrow."

A couple of days later Bill's left hand was a little sore. Each day after that, it got a little more tender. By Thursday his mom suggested he stop for a few days and give his hand a chance to recover. He was frustrated. He couldn't believe it was so hard to learn to milk a stupid cow. He'd learned much harder things, like how to drive a tractor, plow a mule. That had impressed all the guys at school. He was determined to learn how to milk that cow if it took him all year.

Then he remembered his Momma telling him about goals. He picked up his spiral notebook that he used for algebra and went to the inside of the back cover and wrote:

My Goals.

1. Be a soldier.

2. Learn how to milk a cow.

He studied what he'd written for a few minutes and realized he liked what he saw. It gave him a feeling of empowerment. He liked it. He added,

3. Learn to dance.

How to milk a cow school began again on Sunday. Roxanne did more watching than talking. Bill was surprised that his hands weren't hurting so badly now. When he finished, she'd took his seat on the stool and checked to see if he'd milked Bossy until she was dry. He hadn't.

She turned and looked at him sternly, "Bill! You've got to milk her dry or she will stop giving us milk at all."

That was all the motivation he needed.

After two days of success, she told him he could do the evening milking. He was so excited until he realized that he now had talked himself into a new chore.

Chapter 27

On the way to Mamaw Bullock's house on Sunday, Roy couldn't sit still. Charlie pulled in the driveway and they saw Herbert sitting in the swing on the porch. Roy didn't even say hello to him as he burst through the front door. Mamaw was just as excited and they greeted each other joyously. Roxanne had always been envious of their relationship. She often felt when they were together it was like no one else existed. She just followed him into the kitchen chuckling to herself. As Charlie walked into the house, Herbert reached out to Bill to stop him, "Come on, Billy Boy. Let's go down into the woods. The army guys from Dahlonega had their training exercise this week just below the house. Let's go see what we can find. They always lose equipment and I heard machine gun fire a couple of times down below that big tree."

Bill was more excited than Roy. He was about to see how real soldiers played. When Herbert handed him a lard bucket and said, "Take this.

We can pick up the empty shells," Bill couldn't even talk. It was like Christmas to him. As they walked further into the woods, there was a steep incline about fifty yards wide. Bill could see something through the trees. "Is that a railroad track?" he asked.

"Yeah, that's the one that goes from Blue Ridge, through Mineral Bluff and on to Murphy. The other track goes down to Copperhill."

"Oh, is that why they call the crossing Murphy Junction?"

"That's right. Let's head on down to the other side of the tracks," Herbert suggested.

They headed north looking for signs of the soldiers. About a hundred yards later after no results, Bill's excitement was starting to wane. Herbert said, "This is the wrong side. Let's go the other way and see if we have better luck."

They moved fifty feet past their starting point and noticed a group of logs stacked up. On the other side were empty machine gun shells. They quickly filled their bucket. Bill was more excited about the black rings that were on the ground. They were the clips that held the bullets together to form the belt. He began to fill his pockets with them. Herbert complained, "You can't sell those! We can only sell the empty shells."

I don't want to sell them. I want to make them into a belt and keep them," Bill explained.

Herbert just shrugged, "Okay, you can do that too." Then he noticed behind the nest was a hole that appeared to be dug out by some type of animal. When he checked it out, he said, "Look, they put their empty C-Ration cans in this hole."

Bill picked them up and read the labels: Crackers, cheese and peaches. Then he noticed something on a flat rock next to a tree. He held it up and asked, "What is this thing?"

Herbert smiled, "That's the can opener. The Army calls it a P-38."

He took one of the empty cans and demonstrated how it worked on the bottom of the can. When they finally got back to the house, they were in trouble. They'd been gone for more than two hours. Charlie and Roxanne ended up congratulating them once they saw what they'd been up to. They knew Bill lived for that stuff.

She was impressed with the little can opener once Bill showed her how it worked.

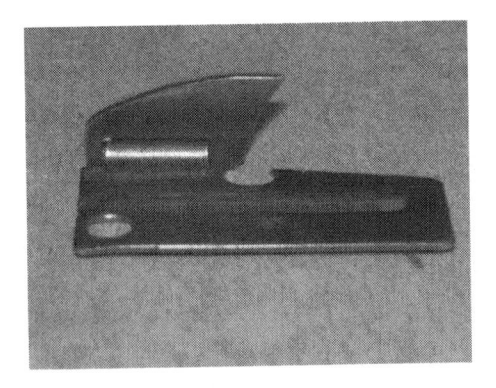

As he played with the P-38 he wished the *Mountain Warriors* could be here with him.

Chapter 28

Bill was nervous as he laid out his clothing on the bed for the canteen. He rushed through supper and finished well before the others. He jumped up, grabbed the milk bucket and practically ran to the barn. Roxanne joked, "Wonder why he's in such a rush?"

"Ah, he just wants to be done before dark. That's all." Charlie responded.

Roy didn't understand at all. It was obvious to him what was happening and he blurted out impatiently, "He's going over to see Jimmy and some old girls!"

His parents burst out laughing, "How do you know that?" his Momma asked.

"I heard 'em at the bus stop talking about dancing and you only dance with girls," he explained.

When Bill finally got to the intersection of Thomas Road and Highway 5, he was disappointed that Jimmy hadn't arrived. He wanted to get to the canteen early so he could dance with Jenny.

He was surprised when Jimmy's father pulled up and yelled out the window, "All aboard for Blue Ridge, Canteen, Cherry Log, and Ellijay." Bill really liked him because he was always joking around with the boys, but he could tell he embarrassed Jimmy.

At the canteen as Jimmy's dad prepared to leave, Bill said, "Sir! Thanks for the ride."

"Anytime young man. Now don't you dance too much," he said grinning as he pulled out.

Bill looked over at Jimmy, "Is your Daddy always so happy? My Dad never laughs."

"You're lucky," Jimmy grumbled.

Bill didn't push it. He understood the way kids felt about their parents. They were the first to enter the canteen that night and didn't recognize any of the kids coming in after them. He leaned over and whispered to Jimmy, "Do any of these girls even go to West Fannin?"

"Nah, they go to East Fannin. They don't have much to do in Morganton, so they come over here."

"Oh, I didn't know that," Bill said.

"Yeah, they usually sit together, but they really like to dance," Jimmy said.

Bill noticed those girls had a lot of records and were the first to start the record player. He moved to a chair in the middle of the room so he could see all the dancers. He was looking for the best ones so he could learn their steps. So far he thought Jenny had them all beat but she was so popular he was embarrassed to ask her for a dance. His plan was to learn to dance so well it would impress her.

He'd been sitting for almost an hour when he decided he needed to give it a try. While he'd been waiting, he'd noticed two girls directly across the floor from him. They, too, were just watching the crowd on the floor. He took a deep breath, walked around the perimeter of the floor until he was in front of the blond. "May I have this dance?"

Her face lit up, "You sure may!"

The song had already started so they both knew it was a fast dance. He took one of her hands and began a step he'd learned on American Bandstand. To his surprise, she responded with the same steps. They finished the song as if they'd danced together for years.

When the music stopped, they were still holding hands. She looked up at him and asked, "How'd you know the moves?"

He decided the best thing to do was just tell her the truth, "I saw it on American Bandstand."

"Arlene and Kenny, right?" she said.

He knew it was Arlene, but had no idea who the guy had been. He answered, "That's right. I'm Bill. What's your name?"

"Betty Lou."

The rest of the night they danced all of the fast songs together. They tried two slow ones but were so clumsy they laughed and sat down. To make conversation Bill asked, "Do you know what Arlene and Kenny's last names are?"

Her girlfriend answered before Betty Lou had a chance, "Arlene Sullivan and Kenny Rossi. My name is Jane and I like to fast dance, too."

All three of them laughed easily as Bill asked, "Would you believe tonight was the first time I've ever fast danced? I was too afraid to ask you. I figured I'd just mess up."

Just as he stopped talking, a new song started. Jane quickly reached out and took his hand, "Well, let's see what you've got."

For the rest of the night they took turns dancing all of the fast songs with Bill. As they were leaving to go home, he learned they were both freshman at East Fannin.

Saturday nights had become the highlight of Bill's weeks. He looked forward to learning new dance steps and meeting new people. Betty Lou and Jane had introduced him to a few of their friends from East Fannin. As the weeks passed by, he became friends with students from both high schools in the area. Because he was shy himself, he felt a kinship to the wallflowers in the room and began to ask some of them to dance.

With the girls help he persuaded some of his friends to join their little group. Jimmy began to kid him that he was building himself a gang. Walking home that night, Jimmy said, "I've noticed the first thing you do every week is to just sit and watch people dance. Then you get up and dance with Betty Lou or Jane and before the night is over you ask some new girl to dance.

If I didn't know better, I'd think you have some kind of battle plan brewing in that mind of yours."

Bill liked the sound of that – **A Battle Plan**. He hadn't thought of it like that before but it fit. He was only trying to build up his confidence. When he danced with people who were as shy as he was, they'd never make fun of him – which was his biggest fear.

Around the end of the school year, the crowd at the canteen became smaller. "Where is everybody?" he asked Jimmy.

"It's prom night."

Bill said, "That's only for juniors and seniors, right?" He'd forgotten all about the big event as he wasn't old enough to attend.

Around closing time, two couples came in. Bill recognized them as seniors at school. They moved to their normal chairs on the west side of the building and everyone stared at the girls' prom dresses. When they got up to dance, all the other couples just stopped and watched them.

They moved to the center of the floor. When the music stopped, everyone clapped. The two boys took small bows and the girls curtseyed. What Bill noticed was both guys were wearing white sports coats with a pink carnation, just like the song. As he watched them dance again, he made up his mind he had to have one of those sports coats for his junior prom.

My Goals.

1. Be a soldier.

2. Learn how to milk a cow.

3. Learn to dance.

4. Get a White Sport Coat, go to Prom.

Chapter 29

When summer arrived, Bill pulled out the gas-powered, 16-inch wide lawn mower. He filled it with gas, checked the oil and pulled the starter rope. On the third pull, it cranked. He felt a sense of pride that he remembered what to do with this wonderful machine. He decided to first mow the grass next to his Daddy's grapevines. It cranked on his first pull and he felt a twinge of excitement. Summer was really here and he was about to mow his first yard.

The grass was higher than normal and as he pushed it into the tall grass, it didn't cut cleanly. He tried pushing slowly and it cut a little better. It still wasn't as good as it had performed the previous summer. He shut it down and turned it up to look at the blades. He was surprised to see they were covered in rust and the cutting edge was blunt and not sharp at all. He studied it for a while and knew it needed to be sharpened, but he didn't have a clue how to go about it. Then he realized the answer. He remembered how sharp his Papaw's axe always was. That was his answer. Papaw could show him how and he wouldn't have to ask his Daddy.

He pushed the mower up into Papaw's yard and he was happy to see him sitting in his rocking chair with his feet up on the post of the porch. "What are you up to, Billy-boy?"

"Papaw, the mower isn't cutting like it used to and I don't know how to fix it."

"Well, let's take it down to the tool house and check it out," Papaw offered.

Once there, they turned the mower over and Papaw immediately identified the problem was with the dull blades. He grabbed a wrench, took the blade off and placed it carefully in a vise. Then he began to teach, "First thing, we need to take off the dings off the backside of the blade. Then let's turn it over and sharpen it just like my axe."

Once finished he turned to Bill, "Now you do the other side."

Bill couldn't believe how easy it was with his Papaw's help. "Thanks! How can I pay you back?"

Papaw grinned, "Well, boy. You can test it on our lawn."

Bill laughed, "Papaw, how'd you learn so much? You know how to fix everything."

"I don't know everything, but if you're a farmer you'll learn how to fix stuff. They are always broken, son."

Bill looked at him with the most serious expression on his face, "Papaw, I'm not going to be a farmer. I'm going to be a soldier."

"Son, you ask a lot of questions when you're a soldier and you'll be a lot smarter than I am when you're my age." Papaw assured him.

Chapter 30

Bill knew something was up as soon as he saw Jimmy at church. "Guess what?" Jimmy said with excitement. "They're going to rebuild Blue Ridge Elementary School! Mr. Haight has the contract. He wants a dozen high school boys to work for him this summer. Daddy's taking me by there Monday morning. You want to go with us?"

Bill couldn't believe it, a real paying job. "Yeah, but I've got to get my parent's permission first."

Everyone moved into the church so Bill had to wait until it was over. He couldn't believe it. Today they had a special music program and they had five songs before the actual service even began. To Bill, it was the longest service in history. When it was finally over, he and Jimmy waited eagerly for their parents in the parking area. It came as a total surprise when his Daddy asked, "Bill, would you like a summer job?"

"Yes, sir."

"Coy tells me he's taking Jimmy to see about a construction job and he's offered to let you go, too, if you're interested." Charlie mentioned. "Son, its hard work, but Mr. Haight pays a good wage and he'll expect a good day's work for it. It's okay with me and your Momma."

"Daddy, I promise I won't embarrass you," Bill said eagerly.

"Don't worry about me, son. Do yourself proud," Charlie said.

Monday at the site location there were already several students there waiting? Bill saw a lot of them were from his school's football team. He didn't know why, but he'd always thought they only played ball and never did any physical labor. After everyone had signed up, Mr. Haight walked straight to Bill. "What's your name, son?"

"Bill Carpenter, sir."

"You ever made mud?" he asked.

Not having a clue what he was talking about, Bill answered, "No, sir. I don't think so."

"Come around the building and I'll show you how."

Once there, Bill noticed a pallet full of bags of mortar mix. They were stacked next to a huge pile of sand. Mr. Haight took a shovel and counted out the shovel loads he threw into a box with a sheet metal bottom. Then he emptied two bags of the mix on top of the sand and with water from a garden hose he mixed the ingredients thoroughly. Then he said, "We call this mortar mix mud. Do you think you can handle this job?"

"Yes, sir."

"Before you answer, I need to make sure you know what comes next. After it's mixed, you need to load it in this wheelbarrow to the bricklayers. Come with me." He took off with Bill towards the side of the building where they were currently laying bricks. He picked up a two foot by two foot piece of ¾ inch plywood and said, "Put their mud on these pieces of wood."

"I can do that, sir." Bill said eagerly.

"I'm not finished, son. You'll be the only one making mud. The hardest part of your job will be replacing the mud the bricklayers use. If you're too slow, they have to stop working and wait on you."

Bill smiled, "I won't let you down, sir."

Mr. Haight stuck out his hand for a shake, "One more thing. They start at 7 a.m. That means you need mud on their plywood before they begin."

Bill nodded quickly, "Sir, I'll come early."

"Son, we're going to do great things with this school building."

For the next couple of months, Bill lived up to his word. At first he had to make a few adjustments because two of the workers were much faster at laying brick than the others. But finally he found a system that worked and he'd resupply the pacesetters first and by the time he finished with the others, he'd add more mud to those two. All summer long he made mud during the week and on Saturday he'd mow lawns. His Daddy would never say it, but he could see his son was becoming a man he was proud of.

Chapter 31

By the end of summer, Bill had saved the money to buy that white sports coat to wear to his junior prom. Now he just had three little things to overcome before the big event. Firstly, he'd need a date; secondly, he'd need a driver's license; and thirdly, he'd need permission to use the family truck. Jimmy had gotten his license the previous spring and had given Bill his old driver's manual so he could study for the written test. He'd done that all summer, but couldn't get up the nerve to ask his Momma to take him to the DMV so he could actually try for his license. He wasn't worried about the driving part of the test, as he'd been doing that on the farm for years. Finally, he decided he needed to just do it. He had twenty-four Saturday nights ahead of him at the canteen in order to find a date. He just hoped she wouldn't mind going in a pickup truck.

The week before school started, he approached his Momma. He explained to her that Jimmy had already gotten his and that Bill had been studying ever since. He begged her to take him.

She smiled, "I wondered when you'd get around to asking. You turned sixteen last April. I'll take your Daddy to work on Friday and we can go then."

"Thank you, Momma."

"Why don't you go read that manual one more time just to be sure you're ready?" she encouraged.

When Friday came, Bill couldn't believe how simple the entire process was for him. As he drove them home, he said, "Momma, that wasn't nearly as hard as I thought it'd be."

"Son, you know why, don't you? You were prepared. If you prepare enough, nothing is too hard."

That fall, his junior year of high school, Bill took Red out for their first hunting trip. It was hard to tell which of them was more excited. It surprised Bill that Red immediately realized they were squirrel hunting and not just taking a walk in the woods. When he later asked his Papaw about that, he laughed and said, "What did you do different?"

"Nothing."

"Now think about it. What did you carry with you?" Papaw quizzed.

"Oh, my shotgun."

"Well there's your answer. Dogs are a lot smarter than people think they are and they're observant, too!"

Bill grinned, "Red really is smart."

Papaw agreed, "That's right. Now when should I plan on getting some squirrel brains for your Mamaw to cook up for me?"

"We'll get you some this Saturday. I promise," Bill said.

Bill, Red and Jimmy fell into their normal fall routine. Bill and Red hunted and Bill and Jimmy walked home together after school. This went on for a few weeks and then something changed with Jimmy. It all came about after the third sock hop of the year. Jimmy was smitten with a new girl, Mary Ann Queen. Bill no longer enjoyed being alone with Jimmy anymore. He was sick and tired of hearing how wonderful she was every time Jimmy had the chance to talk. He decided he'd gone to his last sock hop. The canteen was more to his liking, anyway.

He knew more people there and more people knew him. At the sock hop he only knew a few people because it had always been uncomfortable for him to approach a new girl. Each time he thought about approaching a girl he knew from his classes, his memory flashed back to Roy's experience of being called a poor farmer.

He no longer wore overalls, but he knew they all remembered when he had and he feared they still secretly felt the same way. At the canteen, a lot of the girls just thought of him as a boy who liked to dance.

Chapter 32

With Jimmy in love and spending all his time with Mary, Bill was forced to hitchhike to the canteen by himself. He didn't really mind. If he couldn't get a ride, he'd just walk the three miles. His Daddy bragged he used to walk more than ten miles each Sunday in order to eat dinner with his uncle in Cherry Log.

When Bill arrived, he took his usual seat and began to study the people already there. He noticed a lot of the regulars weren't there, but then he remembered they'd been seniors and had graduated the previous year. Most of them were off in college and the rest must be down in Atlanta finding jobs and working. Good jobs in Fannin County were hard to find. He'd recently heard the Copper Company wasn't hiring anyone this year. He thought about himself and decided if he couldn't get in college, he'd just join the army. Having made that decision, he sat back and started checking out the newbies. There were five girls in the back of the room laughing and dancing with each other. He recognized a couple of them as freshmen and figured the new ones were just replacing the ones who'd moved on with their lives.

He didn't see anyone from his group. He knew Jenny was going to Georgia Tech, but Betty Lou and Jane were just sophomores. When he saw them walking in, he was relieved and then noticed they had two new friends. One was at least a head taller than the others. She had dark hair and beautiful blue eyes. He couldn't take his eyes off of her. He quickly moved towards the group hoping for an introduction. He was introduced to Judy and he stepped closer once he realized they were eye-to-eye. She was as tall as he was. Before he could meet the other girl a slow song started. Bravely he immediately asked Judy to dance. They didn't say a word the entire time they danced. They fit and when their cheeks met, they stayed that way the remainder of the song. Suddenly Bill knew how Jimmy had felt when he met Mary.

An hour later his perfect night fell apart. Two boys came in and Judy introduced one of them as her boyfriend. What was even worse was that Bill recognized Ryan as a football player from West Fannin. He had a couple of classes with him, but Ryan was a jock so didn't give Bill the time of day.

Ryan grabbed his hand saying, "I know Bill. He's in my trig and physics classes."

Minutes later, Bill left the canteen and began walking the long way home. He was depressed and knew he needed the time alone. After about a hundred yards, a car stopped. He was surprised when Mr. McGill said, "Hop in, Bill."

Chapter 33

Ryan had become a fast friend of Bill's after spending a few weeks together at the canteen. In fact, he traded a seat in physics class to be next to him. Bill felt a little guilty because he had worked on this friendship to be close to Judy. Every Saturday he'd get at least two slow dances with her after watching them dance together. He was puzzled, though, because they always kept a large separation between their bodies. One night they were pushed close together as they entered the floor. Bill smiled as he realized Ryan was at least four inches shorter than she was. Then he felt sorry for his friend because the height difference kept him from dancing cheek to cheek with his girl. He knew what it felt like to be embarrassed over something he couldn't control, like being a farmer. He looked around the room and realized Ryan was the only football player there as the others hung out at the McCaysville Tastee-Freeze. It was at that moment that he and Ryan had more in common then he realized.

They were about to take a physics test the following week when Bill pulled out his lucky rock and rubbed it three times.

Ryan was looking at him in puzzlement, "What is that thing?"

"This is my lucky fairy cross," he admitted as he handed it across the aisle to Ryan.

"Where in the world did you get this? Did you make it?" Ryan asked as he studied it intently.

"Nah, I found it on the farm," Bill said.

"Are there more of them?" Ryan asked.

"Plenty. I always find them after we have a big rain storm," Bill said.

Ryan rubbed it, closed his eyes and whispered something to himself. The next day when their tests were returned, Ryan hooted in excitement. "That fairy cross thing works! This is the best grade I've gotten all year. Bill, old buddy, can I find one of those for me?"

"You can try," Bill grinned over at him.

All Ryan could talk about the rest of the week was the fairy cross. "You know Daddy told me you can only find those things in Fannin County. Who would ever believe that it would be a special place?"

Chapter 34

As Bill came out of the woods from squirrel hunting, he noticed a car parked next to the family truck. He threw the three squirrels he'd killed onto the porch and walked in the house to put away his shotgun. Seeing his Momma, he asked, "Whose car is that?"

"That's your friend, Ryan Cheek. He's been waiting for you for about an hour."

Bill looked outside again, "I don't see him."

"Roy took him down to look for fairy crosses," she explained. "And you'd better clean those squirrels before you disappear with your friend."

He quickly cleaned one and handed it over to her. "I promised Papaw some squirrel brains. I'll run these over to him."

She shook her head, "Bill, you never cease to amaze me. The only reason you're taking these to him is so you can hurry and get down to the meadow." She pointed out the way the boys had gone, "They went to the other side of our meadow."

Papaw was on the porch, as usual. Bill ran up and dropped off the two squirrels and handed him the severed head of the other one, "Papaw, I've got to go. We've got company." He ran as fast as he could to the meadow and saw Roy and Ryan in the small stream that bordered it. "What are you guys doing in the branch? Thought you were looking for fairy crosses."

"We couldn't find any. Roy told me he'd seen a red spring lizard. I've never seen one. Have you?" Ryan grinned up at him.

"Look under that old board sticking out of the bank," Bill suggested.

When Ryan turned it over, there it was. It was about six inches long. Bill said, "Cover him back up. He'll be great bait for catching a big old bass this spring. Now, let's go find you a fairy cross."

Bill led them up the old logging road towards a large, bare spot on one of the banks. "Ryan, look where the rain has washed away the dirt. That's where I always find them when I'm looking." All of a sudden, Ryan yelled, "Got one! Man, look! I've got another one."

Roy and Bill stood there laughing at him. Bill teased, "You sound just like Roy on Christmas morning."

Ryan was tickled to death, "This is better than any Christmas I can remember. Can I keep them?"

"You found them. Finders keepers."

"Thank you, Bill. Nobody has ever done anything like this for me before."

Bill left early that evening in order to hitchhike to the canteen. He went where Highway 2 joined Highway 5 (Gravely Gap). Luck was with him yet again as the second car that approached stopped and gave him a ride. He noticed it was easier to get a ride when he was by himself.

He arrived at the canteen before it was time to open and decided he'd stop by the drugstore and get one of those chocolate malts Judy was always going on about.

With the first sip, he agreed with her assessment. As he drank it, he realized he was between a rock and a hard place – he had never felt about a girl the way he did Judy, but Ryan was his best friend. With a sigh, he decided doing nothing was his best option.

When he got back to the canteen, he sat between Betty Lou and Jane. They all sat and watched everyone arrive. Judy came in by herself and Bill wondered where Ryan was. Then Betty Lou asked him, "Bill, when on earth are you going to get up the nerve to ask that girl for a date? It's clear to all of us that you're crazy about her."

He was shocked and embarrassed. He stuttered, "She's really nice and I like her, but she's Ryan's girlfriend. I wouldn't do anything to come between them."

About that time Ryan came in looking around for Judy. Just as they sat down, a slow song came on. She got up, walked straight to Bill and stuck out her hand, "Let's dance."

Betty Lou winked at him.

Chapter 35

"Sweetie, I'm going over and spend some time with Momma and Daddy." Charlie said.

"You eating dinner with them?" She asked.

"Well, you know she won't let me leave until I've eaten at least something."

Roxanne just laughed, "You're got that right."

Later when he got home, he said, "Would you believe Max got married last week?"

"Did he marry that one that broke his heart?" she asked.

"It was Margaret you're talking about, but no. He married a girl from Ellijay named Robin. He's building a house just up from Daddy's on Highway 5. Max asked me if I minded if he asked Bill to help him some," he continued.

"What'd you tell him?" Roxanne asked.

"I told him to go ahead and ask. It would be good experience for Bill," Charlie said as he reached for a leftover biscuit. "I'm guessing Max will end up running him off with all his questions about the army."

She laughed, "Oh my! You're certainly right about that."

"I'll tell Bill at supper," he said.

"No, you won't. He's already left for the canteen."

"You know I think that's been good for him," Charlie said.

"Me, too. I really like the new friends he's making," she said with a smile.

The next day on the way to church, Charlie told Bill about the previous day's events. Bill was so excited he wanted to walk straight to Max's to talk about the job. Roxanne stopped him, "He won't work on Sunday, son. Settle down."

Roy had been listening to the exchange and immediately piped in, "I want to help!"

Charlie nipped that in the bud, "Son, a construction area is a very dangerous place. If you got hurt, it would break Max's heart. You love your uncle, don't you?"

"Yeah, I like him a lot. Okay, Daddy. But can you take me over there sometime so I can see what they're doing?" he pleaded.

"That's a great idea," Charlie said.

Roxanne realized Charlie had solved the problem when she saw the huge grin on Roy's face. She looked over at her husband and winked so he'd know he'd done well.

Bill approached his mother after school, saying, "Momma, I'm going to go see Max's new house and see what he wants me to help him with."

"Sounds good. Tell Roy so he won't be upset with you," she cautioned.

Bill shook his head, "Okay, I'll tell him, but you know he and Daddy watch Howdy-Doody every day after school. He won't miss me."

She just laughed at her oldest son, "Yeah, you're right, but tell him anyway. I'm the one who'll have to listen to his whining when that show goes off."

Bill's visit turned into a new adventure. A month later when Bill showed up after school to work, Max said, "I need you to go to Hampton Hardware and get me some nails. Here's the list."

Bill read it out loud, "Eight penny and ten penny? Will they even know what that is?"

"I'm sure they will." He turned and stuck his hand into the leather tool belt and pulled out a nail. "This is a ten penny." He reached in and grabbed a second one, "And this is an eight penny."

Embarrassed he hadn't known, he said, "How do I get there?"

Max threw him some keys, "Take my car. And hurry up before they close. I'll need them for tomorrow morning."

When he saw the car, he couldn't believe it. It was a brand new Chevrolet and he was getting to drive it! He stood there looking at the car as Max poked him, "Here is some money. You're going to need that."

All Bill could say was, "Oh yeah. I'll be back as soon as I can."

"You're not in that big a hurry. Don't speed, just be careful."

Bill couldn't believe Max and his Daddy were brothers after spending time working with him for a few weeks. Max would give him something to do and would check on him a little later. If he was having a problem, Max would say, "Let me show you an easier way of doing that." He called them tricks of the trade. Bill's Daddy would give him a task and would never even come back to see if he was succeeding. Usually he wouldn't even follow up to see if Bill had actually done as he'd asked. Bill couldn't help himself, he just had to let his Daddy know he was doing a good job. As far as Charlie was concerned, it was over and done with once he'd assigned Bill the job. Whenever Bill felt the need to update his Daddy on his progress, Charlie would simply cut him off, saying, "Sounds like bragging to me."

Max would give him praise, saying, "I couldn't have done it better myself." What made Bill feel the best was when Max would sing his **Happy Song?**

Bill drove the new Chevy more and more over the course of the build. One day it occurred to him that perhaps Max would allow him to borrow the car to take a girl to his junior prom. One day in February, he finally got up the nerve to ask. Max could tell Bill was yearning to ask him a question. After watching Bill make several false starts, Max lost patience and said, "Bill, is there something you want to ask me?"

His face turned red, "I was wondering if I could borrow you care to go to my prom."

Max smiled, "What's your girl's name?"

"I haven't asked anyone yet," Bill admitted reluctantly. "I don't want to ask anyone to go in Daddy's old truck."

"Tell you what. You wash and wax it and you have a deal," Max agreed. Bill couldn't believe his ears. The silence became awkward until Max said, "Let's get this mess cleaned up and go in to supper."

Chapter 36

The next time Max sent him to Hampton's Hardware, Bill decided he'd run across the street to Mull's Department Store and purchase a white sports coat. Then he'd only have one thing left to do before the prom – ask a girl to go. He was having a hard time with that task because Judy was the only one he wanted to attend it with, but he was sure Ryan would be the one taking her.

He thought about taking Betty Lou or Jane, but then everyone would think they were a couple. The same thing applied to any girl in the group at the canteen. He still had a few months left to come up with a solution.

Bill had a mission on Saturday night – find a date, but first he just wanted to dance with Judy. He was waiting for a slow dance. When Ryan and Judy didn't sit with the gang, as usual, he got a feeling something was wrong. Judy told the others they were going to the Swan Drive In to see "*Hound-Dog Man*" with Fabian and Carol Lynley.

She got more excited as Ryan whispered to her, "We need to go."

Judy turned and said, "See you guys next week." Bill was heartbroken and just hoped no one had noticed.

Betty Lou immediately removed that wish by saying, "When on earth are you going to tell her how you feel?"

"What's the point," he asked in frustration. "I'm sure she doesn't feel the same."

"You'll never know unless you ask," she advised wisely.

He just took a seat and began to look around for a girl he could dance with comfortably. He finally noticed a petite blond sitting in the back of the room.

He thought he knew her from some place and he noticed she'd been there for more than an hour and no one had approached her. As he got closer, he recognized her as Connie Johnson. She was in his Latin class and always sat in the last seat in the first row. He hadn't ever spoken to her before. He decided it was time to remedy that, "Connie, would you like to dance?"

"Yes, thank you," she said with a timid smile.

Neither of them said a word as they danced. When the song was over, Bill thanked her and walked away. He'd lost his nerve. After all this time, he still had no idea how to approach a pretty girl. When on earth was he ever going to have a first date?

Bill was rushing to his Latin class on Monday hoping to catch Connie. He was the first there and sat quietly in his seating watching the door. As the students began to file in, he started getting anxious. He remembered his Papaw talking about being as nervous as a cat in a room full of rocking chairs – that's exactly how he was feeling. When Mrs. Saunders walked into the room, he was dejected as Connie still hadn't made her appearance. Four students entered in a group.

He perked up as Connie was amongst them. They were laughing and talking and he figured they were her friends and he knew at that moment today wouldn't be the day he got a chance to talk to her privately.

Bill was walking home from school when Jimmy joined him near Highway 5. It had been weeks since he'd seen him, so it surprised Bill when he just appeared. They walked nearly a half mile without saying a word. That was the first clue – Bill knew something was wrong. Jimmy was just like his Daddy and was always joking and trying to make everyone laugh. Finally Bill just blurted out, "Okay, what's up? You haven't said a word. Spill it."

Jimmy turned towards Bill and had tears welling in his eyes, "Mary's going to Texas. Her Daddy's been promoted and they have to move to Dallas. They leave in two weeks. I just don't know what to do. I can't lose her, Bill."

Immediately, Bill remembered the hurt he'd experienced when Tommy told him he was moving away. He knew exactly how his friend was feeling and even though he wanted to help, he had no idea what to say or do. He couldn't even take him trout fishing because the season didn't open for another month.

He just nodded in silence and they continued walking until they reached Thomas Road. Bill turned and gave him a weak smile, "I'll see you tomorrow, Jimmy."

Jimmy waved and walked away.

Bill walked into homeroom the next morning and was surprised to see everyone standing around talking at once. The girl seated next to him leaned over and asked, "Have you heard? Mrs. Saunders died last night."

"Was it a car accident?" he asked.

"No, she died from the cancer she had. I thought you knew," the girl explained. "Cancer was why she had such a deep voice."

Bill had thought her voice was like that because she was old, but he figured it wouldn't do any good to say it out loud. When he got to his Latin class, there was an older women at the desk. She made an announcement to the class on what had happened and then quickly exited the room. Bill seized on this opportunity and decided he'd talk to Connie.

When he stood to move towards her, he saw she was laughing with her four friends and having a good time. He didn't have the confidence to approach her – once again.

Mrs. Saunders' death was a blessing for the class. The new substitute teacher continued to use her lesson plan, but she was reviewing the curriculum Mrs. Saunders had covered months before. No one in the room told her and when she gave the same test they'd had before, everyone agreed it was a special gift from Mrs. Saunders.

The teacher seemed pleased at how well they all did on the test. It was only a few weeks until the end of the school year, so no one learned any new material, but they enjoyed their time together.

Chapter 37

Bill was sitting in his usual chair as he thought about his dilemma. He had the sports coat and a car to drive, but no date. He thought he'd have been able to convince Connie to go to the prom with him, but he'd been too late. It didn't bother him that much because he really only wanted to go with Judy anyway. He'd never felt like this about anyone before. The first time he'd met her, he was hooked and the more he was around her, the more intense his feelings were. He had been naïve to assume that he could just wait for her and Ryan to break up; but after weeks of watching them, he realized they were getting closer, not breaking up. Frustrated and not seeing a solution, he decided at that moment to just forget about even going to his junior prom. He'd been twisting and turning in that old metal chair as he'd pondered his problem. Betty Lou had been watching and she instinctively knew what he was fretting about.

Finally she grabbed his hand, saying, "Let's dance." It was a fast dance and one of his favorite songs and he soon seemed to have snapped out of his depression. When the song finished, she moved him away from the group so they could talk.

"Bill, you're never going to get a date with Judy if you don't ask. It's clear she's the only one you want to be with for the prom. I have a proposition for you. I'll be your date this year. At least that way you can get a few dances with her. In return, next year I'll be a junior and you can be my date. What do you say? Is it a deal?"

The more he was around her, the more he felt of her as the sister he'd never had and he knew she felt exactly the same. He stuck out his hand, "It's a deal."

She grinned, "Then we'd better go dance. We're going to need all the practice we can get."

Prom day had finally arrived. Bill picked up Betty Lou at her home in Morganton. The parking lot was full as they arrived at the high school and she whispered to him as they walked into the gym, "Look! It's so beautiful. I wonder how long it took them to decorate."

"I think they've been working on it all week," he said as he looked around with interest.

"Did you help?" she asked.

"Nah, no one asked me," he admitted as they took a seat on the bleachers about midway up so they could see the full effect of all the hard work that had gone into transforming the gym into something magical.

Bill began looking around as Betty Lou said, "There they are in the middle of the bleachers on the other side."

He was embarrassed that she knew him so well. She forced him to dance several dances and later in the evening Judy approached them and asked if it was okay if she danced with Bill. When they'd finished their slow dance, Bill came back to his seat and pointed to his watch.

"It's getting late and I promised your Dad I'd get you home before midnight."

She knew her Dad had just been teasing, but she didn't want to embarrass him as she figured he was eager to get away from Judy and Ryan. On the way home she said, "I'm going to be on our prom committee next year. I've got a lot of good ideas from this one." Bill was thinking to himself as she babbled on, if you don't have someone special as your date, it's just another dance. He didn't think he'd ever find that person.

At that moment he decided he'd wasted enough time mooning over girls. He'd use every moment from here on out learning how to be the best soldier he could be.

Chapter 38

Bill returned Max's car keys and thanked him on Monday after school. Max waited patiently for Bill to tell him all about it, but when he failed to do so, he finally asked, "Did you have fun? What was it like?"

"It was in the gym. They'd decorated it like a fairy tale or something. Lots of castles and knights. I guess all proms are like that. Was yours?"

Max shrugged, "How would I know? I never went. I quit school in the ninth grade to go to work. Daddy needed help supporting the family."

Bill didn't know what to say. He blurted out, "But you liked the army, right?"

"Believe it or not, I really liked it. I've asked myself why I got out at least a hundred times. They teach you a skill and then let you do it. When I quit school, I didn't have any skills that would earn me money. I just knew how to farm. Don't you ever even think about quitting school, boy." Max cautioned.

Bill shook his head vehemently, "I won't, I promise.

I want to be a soldier like you. Can you help me?"

"Oh yeah. That'll be fun. Let's start right now, private. We'll begin with police call. That's what the army calls picking up trash and making the place look neat. Would you believe they even park all their vehicles in a straight line equal distances apart?"

Bill smiled, "Uncle Max, you're the best."

"Be sure and tell your Mamaw that. Now let's get to work."

Max introduced Bill to a new facet of army life every time they worked together. Finally, Bill asked, "What was your rank, Uncle Max?"

Max took the opportunity to explain how it all worked, saying, "I was an E-3 on the pay scale and I wore PFC stripes. I was about to get promoted when I decided to leave."

"What does E-3 mean?" Bill asked, fascinated.

"The E means enlisted and the 3 determines what my pay was. Officers would be O-3. That means the 3 for him would be the rank of Captain."

Bill asked, "Do officers get better pay?"

Max laughed, "Well, what do you think? I'm guessing it's about ten times as much."

"Is it hard to become an officer?" Bill asked.

"That I don't know," Max admitted. He gave Bill a lot more information over the coming weeks, but the difference between enlisted and officer had made a significant impact on the little warrior.

Chapter 39

Spring had arrived again and Bill thought it was great. The grass was growing and mowing lawns to earn money would keep him busy. He didn't even need help this year to get everything ready for the season. He removed the blade and did as his Papaw had taught him. Once finished, he rolled it outside of the tool shed so he could admire his work. He smiled in satisfaction – so this is what Mamaw meant when she told him about pride of accomplishment. He really didn't need anyone to tell him he'd done a good job, it was obvious. As he put the blade back on, he realized he needed a mentor about being a soldier. Good guidance, like his Papaw had given him before, would go a long way towards his success. Uncle Max had relayed all he knew, but Bill realized Max didn't know anything about becoming an officer. In order to be successful, he needed someone to fill that role. One day he'd like to feel that same sense of accomplishment by being an officer in the United States Army. As he sat there smiling, Roy approached asking, "What are you doing? Can I help?"

"I'm getting the mower ready to cut grass," Bill replied.

"Can I cut grass, too? I'm big now," Roy asked eagerly.

"I don't know. That lawnmower is dangerous. If you get your foot underneath it, it could cut off your toes," Bill said in a serious tone. He feared Roy was only nine years old and far too young to do that kind of work unsupervised.

"Ah, you're just teasing me. If I stay way back and push it straight, my feet won't get anywhere near the mower. I'll stay safe, I promise," Roy said, pleading his case.

Bill looked over at him with a glare, "If I let you mow some, you can't tell Momma."

Roy's eyes got big, "No way. We can't tell her, she still thinks I'm just a baby."

Bill burst out laughing. "Okay, here's what we'll do. We can take turns until you get used to it. I'll let you mow where it's flat and easier to push."

Roy was ecstatic, "That's a great idea. Can we get started now?"

Bill nodded, "Let's go mow around the grapevines."

Roy smiled, "Momma can't see us down there, can she?"

"I'll mow the area next to the garden first and then you can mow behind the smokehouse. That way she won't be able to see you."

The plan worked great. When Roy finished his section, Bill told him he'd mow the yard in front of the house and their mother wouldn't suspect a thing.

Roy winked, delighted that he'd been given the opportunity to show Bill what he was capable of, "It'll be our secret."

"Why don't you go in the back door while I'm mowing?" Bill suggested. As he mowed the front, he decided it would be a lot safer if he didn't show Roy how to actually start the lawnmower until next year when he was a little older.

Chapter 40

He was at the canteen early because he'd caught the second car that passed him. He didn't like being the first to arrive. He looked at his watch and saw it was almost 8 o'clock. If none of his friends had arrived within the next few minutes, he'd just hitchhike back home. Just as he stood to leave, Betty Lou ran up whispering, "Ryan and Judy broke up last week!" Before she could elaborate further, he looked up and saw Judy walking across the floor. She came right to him and stuck out her hand, "Let's dance."

It was a fast dance, but he didn't care. He was dancing with Judy. For the next ninety minutes they danced every song together. It seemed strange because neither of them said a word. Bill was afraid if he opened his mouth, he'd break the spell. Walking back to their seats after a slow dance, Judy said, "Ryan and I decided to call it quits." She smiled at him, "Do you know anyone who might be willing to take me to see *A Summer Place* tomorrow?"

"*The Summer Place*" with Sandra Dee and Troy Donahue

Bill smiled and ducked his head, "I might know a few. What kind of guy are you looking for?"

"I'd really like one as tall as me and who loves to dance. Bring anyone to mind?"

"Not sure. If it's okay with you, I can take you to that movie," he said as casually as he possibly could.

She squeezed his hand, "Then it's a date."

Bill wished he had a car so he could take her home that evening, but he didn't.

Before they left, he asked her to write down directions to her house. The movie would start at 1 o'clock.

Betty Lou and Jane hadn't danced much that night. They'd been standing in the corner watching the two of them. It had been hilarious watching how they both were so captivated and not even aware of another person in the room.

Sunday morning after Bill had milked the cow, he raced back to the house. He thrust the bucket at his mother saying, "I need to go see Uncle Max, but I'll be back in time for church."

She stopped him, "Here, take this sausage biscuit with you. I won't let you miss breakfast."

He gobbled it down as he ran to Max's. When he ran up into the yard he didn't see the car. He pounded on the door and Robin asked when she opened the door, "What's wrong, Bill?"

"I need to borrow Max's car today. I have a date."

She shook her head sadly, "I'm so sorry, Bill. Max is down in Atlanta and won't be back until Wednesday."

He was devastated, but remembered his manners, "Thank you ma'am. I need to get home and go to church."

She called out as he walked away, "I'm sorry he's not here. I'll tell him you came to see him."

Bill ran even faster home. "Momma! I need a favor. Do you think Daddy will loan me the truck today so I can take Judy Mull to the matinee in McCaysville?"

She smiled, "What time is the show?"

"One o'clock," he said hopefully.

She walked into the living room, "Charles, Bill needs the truck at noon. We can walk home from church."

Charlie didn't know what to say, so just nodded in agreement. He could tell when his wife meant business, "Oh, okay. It's not that far anyway."

She turned to Bill and winked, "Go get dressed, young man."

Bill couldn't believe how easy that had been. After church, he drove straight to Judy's. On the way he began to worry that she wouldn't like riding in an old pickup truck.

The closer he got to her home, the more apprehensive he became. As he drove up into her driveway, he couldn't believe his eyes. In front of him sat a Ford pickup truck very similar to his Daddy's Chevy.

Judy was sitting on the front porch swing when she saw him drive up. She immediately ran down the steps and opened the passenger door before he even had time to get out of the truck. She looked at him apologetically as she said, "We have to hurry or we won't make it in time. Why don't we go the Mineral Bluff Highway? It's shorter."

He didn't want to admit it, but he had no idea how to go that route. Finally he ducked his head and mumbled, "I don't know how to do that."

"Just go up to Lakewood, make a right and stay on that road," she said as she settled in comfortably on the front seat."

Relieved she hadn't made fun of him, he grinned at her, "Okay, but don't you dare get us lost, young lady!"

She laughed, "Now would I do that to you?"

"Well, it is our first date," he said shyly.

She slid across the seat and kissed him on the cheek, "Quit talking and drive. I really want to see this movie."

Bill smiled, "Know what my Daddy would say to my Momma right now? He'd look at her and say 'Yes, boss.'"

She just chuckled, "Sounds like your Daddy's a smart guy."

"Yes, boss."

She punched him in the side and said, "Drive." They were comfortable now, both of them relieved it wasn't awkward. When they finally got to the theater, he couldn't find a space to park. Judy had him drive down the street to the ballpark. Once they were out, she grabbed his hand, saying, "Let's run. It's ten minutes before it starts."

Her hand in his gave him a warm feeling. He couldn't believe how fast she could run, but he knew he could keep up with her easily.

It was his first time in this particular theater and he was impressed at how large it was. He was staring at the ceiling when she grabbed his hand saying, "There are two seats in the third row. Let's go."

He could see why she was so intense as almost every seat had already been taken. Evidently this was going to be one great movie as the entire town had turned out to see it. As they sat, the previews began. He would look over at her and smile as she was enthralled with everything on the screen. When the movie was over, she kept talking about how wonderful it had been.

TASTEE FREEZE
McCaysville, Georgia

She was surprised into silence when Bill turned into the Tastee-Freeze. As they ate, she talked nonstop about the star of the movie, Troy Donahue. He figured he'd counter her with how sweet and cute he thought Sandra Dee was. She frowned at him in annoyance, saying, "So are you saying you prefer blondes?"

He just laughed in satisfaction and said nothing.

A couple miles later she finally said, "Aren't you going to say anything?"

"My Uncle Max told me when you find yourself in a hole, stop digging."

She laughed out loud, "You know the menfolk in your family seem to be pretty smart." She slid across the seat to sit closer and just before they got to Morganton she had him take her to the church and drop her off there explaining she was teaching a class that afternoon.

On the way home, he couldn't have been happier. The first date with the girl of his dreams had gone perfectly.

Chapter 41

Walking with Roy to the bus stop, Bill couldn't stop thinking about his date with Judy. The wait had been worth it as she was just as wonderful as he'd thought. He had no idea why she and Ryan had broken up, but he was glad they had. Only problem was he now had to see Ryan at school every day until the end of the year. How on earth was that going to work? Would Ryan be furious that Bill had taken Judy out? He mumbled to himself as he worked himself up into a frenzy, "What on earth would the Mountain Warriors do?"

Roy overheard him, "What's wrong? Are we in trouble? If I did something, I don't remember what it was."

"Nah, I got myself into this mess all on my own, little brother," Bill said shaking his head.

Bill couldn't concentrate in any of his classes as he was dreading seeing Ryan. It was finally time for physics and he walked with increasingly slow steps. Ryan always sat next to him in that class. As he sat, Ryan looked over eagerly, "Bill, those fairy crosses really work! I'm doing so much better in this class."

Bill was surprised and said, "Think it could be you're actually studying more?"

Ryan grinned. Then he blurted out, "You know, Judy and I decided to call it quits. I know you like to dance with her, but why don't you ask her out? She loves movies. You should take her to one before she moves."

All Bill heard was 'before she moves'. It hit him like a ton of bricks and before he could ask Ryan to elaborate, Mr. Haymore came in and announced a pop quiz. By the time class was over, he had decided it would be smarter to ask Betty Lou about the details of the move instead of Ryan. She'd know more about it than he would anyway.

Bill drove the family truck Saturday night and got to the canteen early so he'd find a good parking place. His plan was to talk to Betty Lou first to see what he could find out. Then he'd spend the rest of the night dancing with Judy; and hopefully, get to take her home. When Betty Lou walked through the door, he jumped up and pulled her to the opposite side of the room so they'd have some privacy. He asked what she knew.

"I was going to tell you last week, but she came in before I had a chance. Her Daddy is a Baptist Minister and has been asked to pastor a large church down near Atlanta. They'll move as soon as school is out. I'm so sorry, Bill," Betty Lou said sympathetically.

He just hung his head in disbelief. "At least I might be able to take her home tonight so we can talk about it. Betty Lou, I've waited so long, I don't want to lose her."

She was dreading giving him even worse news, but said, "Bill, she won't be here tonight. The church is giving him a farewell party tonight and she had to attend that."

"Ryan told me she was moving and I was hoping I'd get a chance to talk to her about it. He actually suggested I take her to the movie on a date," Bill said.

"I think everyone knows how much you liked her. It's such a shame she's leaving now when she knows how you feel about her," Betty Lou said. She moved back across the room to their friends and left Bill sitting quietly by himself. It was obvious he just needed to be alone.

After giving it another hour to see if she'd show up, he gave in and decided to head home. All the way he beat himself up over how stupid he'd been not to ask her out sooner. He just had no idea what to do. As he drove past the Mercier's apple house, he decided to drive to her church and tell her how he felt. By the time he got to Morganton, it was getting late. As he got out of the truck, he noticed a crowd coming out and going home. He maneuvered as quickly as he could through the people leaving, looking for Judy. He didn't know what her parents looked like, so finding her was his only option. He searched relentlessly, but she wasn't there. He took his time driving home.

Chapter 42

Freshly showered and dressed, Bill planned to go see Judy right after church. As they began the drive from church, trouble began. Roy always had to sit in Roxanne's lap because the truck only held three people. He didn't like how it made him look like a baby and made it known every time they went somewhere. As they began the drive, Bill quickly realized they were on the way to his Mamaw and Papaw Bullock's house – not home. He couldn't believe how discouraged he felt and tried to rationalize it wouldn't have been proper to just show up at Judy's house. He was silent the entire trip.

Roy jumped out immediately and ran to see his Mamaw. Papaw was on the front porch whittling as they all got out. Bill looked around and when he didn't see Herbert, asked, "Where's Herbert?"

"You haven't heard? He and that Arp boy joined the army a couple of weeks ago," said Papaw. "The only job he could find around here was at Reece's Grocery as a bagboy. He wanted me to tell you those ranger boys were back a while ago."

"Thanks, I'll go look and see what I can find," Bill said quietly. He went and got the lard bucket from right where they'd left it last time. He felt lucky they used the same place for the machine gun nest and in just a few minutes he'd collected all the spent ammunition and clips. He walked back up to the house and sat on the tailgate of the truck while putting the ammunition back in a belt. Once finished, he had a belt almost six feet long. His timing was perfect as his mother called him in to eat dinner.

The next week was test week so he studied and prepared. Saturday morning after milking the cow, he got out the lawnmower and began to cut the lawn. When he finished, he told his Momma he was going to cut his Mamaw and Papaw's lawn. She smiled, "That's a nice thing you're doing son. Be careful."

Charlie moved from the front porch inside with Roy to watch television. He looked over at Roxanne and asked, "What's got into that boy? He's been busy all day."

"Charlie Carpenter, are you that naïve?"

"What are you talking about?" he asked.

"What day is it? Where does he go on Saturday night," she reminded him.

"The canteen? Oh! He wants the truck tonight," he said, finally clueing into her reasoning.

"Yes, and if you're expecting to eat the rest of the week, you won't tell him no," she warned.

He just grinned, "Yes, boss." He turned back to the television, talking to himself, 'Lord, I love that woman.'

Roy looked up, "What did she do?"

"She didn't do anything, son. She's just being your Momma." he replied.

At the canteen, Bill sent up a prayer as he entered that Judy would be there. He could see her as soon as he came through the door. She was standing with her friends. He leaned against the wall where she couldn't see him until the first slow song came on. It happened to be one of her favorites, so he approached her smiling and asked her to dance. When her friends saw him coming, they moved aside so Bill and Judy could dance. Judy whispered, "I missed you last week."

Bill remained silent until it was over. He walked her over to the opposite side of the room and asked her, "Why didn't you tell me you were moving away?"

She teased, "I didn't think you'd care."

"I care too much. I don't want you to leave," he admitted.

"It's not like I'm falling off the face of the earth," she said, trying to keep it light.

"Atlanta is a hundred miles away. How will I get to see you?"

"I'll come up. My brother Randy lives up here. I have a lot of relatives I can come see," she said.

"I don't know. You'll get down there and find you a rich city boy," he said, expressing his worst nightmare. He had waited so long for this girl that he felt like he was in agony. But it was awkward. He hadn't even come close to telling her how he felt.

She laughed and said, "I'll tell them they'd better watch out because I have a boyfriend in the mountains."

"Are you saying I'm your boyfriend?" he asked hopefully.

"That's what I'm saying and I like it that way," she replied, squeezing his hand.

"You realize that means I'm obligated to take you home tonight, right?" Bill said with a smile.

"I agree with that."

"Also guess that means we'll be going to the movies tomorrow. What's playing?" he asked.

"I have no idea and I don't really care. We'll be together," she said as they walked off the dance floor with their arms around each other.

Bill ducked his head to keep from bursting out laughing when he caught Betty Lou's eyes and she was jumping up and down, saying, "I told you so!"

Chapter 43

All Bill could think about was the week ahead of him. It would be his last week as a Junior at West Fannin, but what was more important was Judy's move next Saturday to Atlanta. She'd promised to go out with him one more time before she left, so they had planned on Friday night. School would take care of itself. What he needed to focus on was making their date as special as possible. Around midnight it finally clicked into place. When he'd first met her, she'd been all excited about going to the Swan Drive-In. He had never been, so he was concerned that he'd look like a fool by not knowing how it all worked. Finally after wrestling with the problem, he fell asleep.

At the bus stop, Uncle Max drove by and honked his horn. Bill waved back and then had an idea. He'd ask Max to borrow the car for Friday. Judy would love it. After school, he ran to Max's, eager to ask permission. He had come up with the idea of offering to cut Max's lawn all summer if he could use the car for just that one night.

Max laughed when he asked, "Of course you can. Sounds like you really like this girl. What's her name?" Max was amused at how nervous Bill was about it.

"Judy Mull. She's moving to Atlanta on Saturday, but she promised to keep in touch."

Max identified with Bill's problem. The girl who'd broken his heart when he'd been in the army had moved to Atlanta as well.

She'd gotten married a year before he left the service. Max said, "I'll make you a deal. You can have the car if you mow the lawn twice this summer." He stuck out his hand, "Is it a deal?"

Bill latched onto Max's hand, pumping with all his might, "You bet it's a deal."

Bill didn't even bother changing his clothes before grabbing up the milk bucket Tuesday afternoon. Roxanne looked up in surprise, asking, "Hey! Where are you going with that?"

"Momma, I've got a date Friday night with Judy. Max said I could use his car if I got his lawn mowed before then. If I milk the cow now, I can get it done before dark."

She just looked at him, all the while remembering his first day at school. He was just as excited today as he'd been way back then. She smiled, "Put that bucket back where you found it. I'll do the milking tonight. You go take care of your end of the deal with Max. By the way, when do I get to meet Judy?"

All of a sudden he was tongue-tied. He didn't know whether to tell her Judy was moving. "I don't know, Momma, but I know you'll like her when you do."

"Go get out of those good clothes and mow that lawn," she said with a smile. She loved how responsible her oldest child had become. He always did what he said he would. Now, maybe if only some of that could rub off on Roy.

At Judy's house on Friday evening, Bill was relieved to see there wasn't a Ford pickup in the driveway. Judy ran to greet him as he exited the car.

"It's you! I was worried. I thought more people were stopping by to see Daddy. Let's get out of here before anyone else shows up."

As they drove, she asked, "When did you get a car? It's really nice."

"It's not mine. It belongs to Uncle Max. He bought it when he was in the army. When I join, I'll have a nice one, too," Bill boasted.

She was surprised at his statement. "When did you decide to do that?"

He grinned, "Way back in elementary school. Some of us local boys used to play army all the time. We loved it. We called ourselves the Mountain Warriors." He was amused at himself as he told her the story. It was such a good time in his life.

Crossing the Blue Ridge Dam, she said, "You never cease to surprise me. Where are we going?"

"Well, I know you love the movies so I thought we'd go to the Swan Drive-In in Blue Ridge," he told her. They both stayed quiet for a few minutes. As they went around Dead Man's Curve, Bill decided he'd better admit to her he actually knew nothing about drive-ins.

"Judy, I'm sorry, but I've never been to one before, so I have no idea how it all works."

She laughed, "Don't worry. I'll walk you through it. It's not hard. You pay at the entrance and then to the back row of speakers. Park so the speakers are beside my window."

He was relieved and followed her instructions exactly. When she hung the speaker on her window, she turned and said, "Bill, promise me you'll always be this honest with me. Most boys feel they can't let girls find out they don't already know everything. You have no idea how refreshing it is to know you have the same insecurities as I do. So thank you for that."

He blushed, "I guess you might regret that in the future. Let me ask you a question. Why did you pick all the way in the back to watch the movie?"

She didn't say a word. She just slid across the seat and gave him their first real kiss.

Bill awoke happy on Saturday. The most wonderful girl in the world liked him and what was really great was she liked him just as he is – a plain country boy. Feeling the warm glow of new love, he couldn't help but sadden at the thought that today was moving day for her. A hundred miles away could be a thousand and it wouldn't make any difference. They were going to be worlds apart. He couldn't even express how he was feeling. Once he'd gone to a funeral of a young man and he'd overheard the man's wife say to his momma that she felt like she had a hole in her heart and didn't know what she would do. Bill now knew exactly how that woman had felt. What could he do? He didn't have a car, she didn't have a car and there was no way they could see each other as often as they'd like. He would just have to stop himself from thinking about her all the time and maybe that would help. At breakfast, he asked, "Daddy, when are we going to mow the meadow? Don't we need hay?"

"Son, glad you're so concerned. I'd planned on doing it this week, but they say it's going to rain tomorrow. I'll ask Frank to do it Wednesday or Thursday."

Then he looked over at Roy and winked, "You old enough to stack hay this year?"

"Yes, daddy. Can we start today?" Roy asked, squirming in his seat.

"No, son. You have to cut the hay first. Maybe next Saturday," Charlie said.

Bill left to milk the cow, then got out the mower and began to take care of the yard. He discovered staying busy seemed to be keeping his mind off of Judy. He went in and told his Momma he was going up to mow his grandparent's lawn and headed that way. By noon, he was finished – which left him hours before he could go to the canteen. He went over and mowed Mrs. Griggs' lawn even though she wasn't home. By the time he finished, he was exhausted.

He thought about not going to the canteen at all that night, but soon realized he'd have to explain why he wasn't going to his Momma. It would be a lot easier to just go. Once there, Betty Lou and Jane met him at the door, asking "Is she gone?"

He nodded, "Yeah, but said she'd come back to see her brother. She'll let me know when."

Betty Lou demanded, "You'd better bring her here. Promise you will?"

He nodded and took a seat, in no mood to dance. After he'd stayed long enough to appease his mother, he went home. After milking the cow the next morning, he got ready for church. His Momma asked, "Bill, do you want the truck today?"

"No, not today," he said frowning.

She was shocked, "Are you sure? We won't need it today."

"Momma, did I tell you Judy's Daddy is a preacher? He's the minister of the church in Morganton and was asked to move to a much larger church in Atlanta. They moved yesterday."

Roxanne just looked at him, "Oh, so that explains why you were so busy yesterday."

"Yes, ma'am. Why don't we go to Mamaw Bullock's after church? You know how much she likes to see Roy," he suggested.

She reached over and patted his back, trying to express to him she understood what he was feeling without actually saying anything, "Son, I think that's a great idea."

Chapter 44

The meadow was still fresh with dew when Charlie, Max, Roy and Bill gathered there on Saturday morning. Frank had cut the hay on Wednesday so Max could rake it into long rows in time for today. Papaw wasn't helping this year as he'd fallen and bruised his shoulder. When Charlie pulled the tractor up to the first row, Bill started to climb aboard. "Not this time, Bill, I need you to take your Papaw's place," said Charlie. While the tractor sat there idling, he instructed Roy to climb up and get comfortable. "Push in the brake with your right foot and the clutch there on the left with that foot," Charlie instructed as he put it into gear. "Take your foot off the brake and slowly ease up on the clutch." As the tractor began to move, Charlie said, "Now, push in the clutch." The tractor stopped.

Roy whooped with joy, "Daddy, I did it!"

"You did a fine job, son. We're going to be behind you throwing hay on the trailer, so when we get all of it picked up off the ground, I'll need you to ease the tractor and trailer ahead of us by about twenty-five feet. I'll tell you when to stop."

Bill was watching them, remembering his Daddy giving him the exact same instructions when he'd been that age. He just chuckled seeing the smile on his Daddy's face when Roy did exactly what he'd been told to do.

He wondered if he'd ever get to teach his son this skill. Then he wondered if soldiers would even do that.

The spell was broken when he heard Max call out to him, "Hey, Private! Get to work." Bill loved it when Max called him Private or Sergeant.

After about eight times with Roy doing really well, Charlie took over and drove the tractor up to the three haystacks. Roy quickly moved to the center pole of the closest haystack and began packing down the hay as they threw it.

That night after dinner, Roy crashed while in front of the television. Charlie didn't say a word, but just carried the exhausted child to bed.

Every day after that Roy asked his Daddy when they'd cut hay again. After a couple of weeks, Charlie complained to Roxanne as they got into bed, "That boy is worse than Bill. He just keeps bugging me about cutting hay."

"That's good news, isn't it? I'd love it if he grew up to be as responsible as his brother, wouldn't you?" she said with a frown.

"Well, smarty pants, when do you plan on teaching him how to milk that cow?" Charlie threw out.

"Bill already knows how to milk the cow."

"No, I meant Roy," Charlie said.

"Oh for goodness sake. Let that boy drive the tractor a few more times and he'll be ready to learn," she said.

"Woman, how'd you get so smart?" he said as he turned over.

"Self-defense," she said. "I'm surrounded by three men."

"Yes, boss," he said grinning at the wall.

Chapter 45

Bill had tried to stay busy and keep his mind off of Judy for weeks. He'd spent a lot of his time with Max and his Papaw. Going to Papaw's and working with his mule was the most enjoyable as Roy hated that mule and avoided it like the plague. After spending so much time with it, he was really getting good at plowing and using the sled. He could take the sled in the woods where the truck wouldn't go and because of that he'd almost cut enough firewood to get the family through the winter months. He smiled at the neatly stacked wood, remembering how his Mamaw had suggested he take pride in his finished work. One day he'd thank her for how her advice had freed him from constantly seeking his Daddy's approval. He decided he'd do it once he met his goal of becoming a soldier.

After weeks of not hearing anything, today when he got home his mother handed him a letter.

.Dear Bill,

We're finally settled in our new home. I'm sorry it's taken me so long to write, but I wanted to have good news when I did. We are going to be coming to Blue Ridge to visit my brother the week of the fourth of July. I'll write later to let you know the exact dates when I know them so you can see what movie will be showing at the Swan. I miss dancing with you and seeing our friends at the canteen. I've been begging Daddy to let us stay through the weekend, but he's not sure he can because he has to be back for Sunday services. Tell everyone I said hello and pass along my address to them if they're interested. Love you,

Judy

Bill hadn't been to the canteen since she'd moved and he had no idea what to say to Betty Lou and the others. He was the first person through the door on Saturday night. He tried to help the adults as they were opening up. His friends bombarded him with questions the moment they saw him. He had to chuckle at how eager they were to hear about Judy, so he quietly handed out pieces of paper with her address written on them.

He told them she'd be up for the holiday weekend, but might not get to stay through Saturday. After catching everyone up, he danced a few fast numbers with Betty Lou and Jane. He just didn't feel right about dancing a slow one.

He was a little surprised later that night when Ryan came in calling out, "Where have you been? I've been here every Saturday trying to tell you my great news. I was telling my uncle how you wanted to be a second lieutenant and he called a friend of his and he told me about NGC. It's a military school in Dahlonega. I really like what he told me about the school. What do you think?"

"Sounds great. I like it," Bill said eagerly.

Ryan grinned, "Why don't we apply and be roommates?"

Bill smiled, "We'd better go find some more of those fairy crosses for good luck."

Ryan stuck out his hand, "Let's shake on it. Is it a deal?" Late in June Bill got another letter from Judy.

Dear Bill,

Another update and I think you'll like it. I know I do. With the 4th being on Monday, Daddy plans to drive us up that morning and they will go home on Wednesday. The good news is I'm staying with my brother and he will take me home on Sunday. That way I can go with you to the canteen. I sure do miss our slow dancing together. Oh yeah, I'm not sure if I told you where my brother lives. He's in the small house across the street from Reece's Grocery Store. You might already know that, but I just wanted to make sure.

Your girlfriend,

Judy

Bill loved every word of the letter; but now he had a problem. He knew he didn't have enough money to last the entire week. He made a list of how he could earn it. Mrs. Griggs was at the top of his list because she always paid more. He had a total of five yards he could mow, but he was afraid that wouldn't be enough. He got an idea of how he could get Roy to help him. He pulled him aside on Sunday saying, "Roy, how do you feel about going on a treasure hunt?"

Roy's eyes went wide, "When can we start?"

"As soon as you change out of those church clothes," Bill said.

Roy didn't say another word. He just took off to change. While he was gone, Bill grabbed an old Coke crate out of the tool shed. He thought about his old Grits route and where he'd seen the most empty bottles along the way. When Roy began to lose interest, Bill would praise him, saying he always found the most bottles. It worked and every single day Roy looked for a new location in which to find empties. Bill hadn't told him he could get a two cent return fee on each bottle at McAfee's Store and by the end of the week they had enough for ten dollars. Mr. McAfee had given him two half dollars. Those two large coins satisfied Roy as he'd never earned so much money in his life and couldn't believe his luck. When he showed them to Roxanne, she gave Bill a glare. When Roy went outside to show his coins to his Daddy, Bill quickly explained how he'd been desperate to earn enough money to cover his expenses while Judy was in town. She hugged him and told him she was proud of him for working so hard. "Money is really tight for us right now and will be until your Daddy sells the calves in the fall."

"Thank you, Momma. Can I help?" Bill asked, feeling guilty.

"No, son. Keeping Roy busy helps more than you will ever know," she said with a smile.

Monday evening Bill drove to Judy's brother's house. The driveway was so full of cars and trucks he had to park on the street. Walking towards the house, he saw someone pushing an old lawn mower while her Father was trimming the hedge closest to where he'd parked. Judy and another woman were sitting on the porch, talking as they watched the men work. Judy turned to her mother as he walked up the steps, "Mother, this is Bill."

"Nice to meet you Mrs. Mull," he said. Then he grinned and asked, "Do all mothers supervise while their men work?"

She raised her eyebrow in surprise while hiding her instinctive smile, "Oh, it's hard work, but it needs to be done."

He laughed out loud, "You sound just like my Momma."

Mrs. Mull acknowledged the compliment, saying, "Well then, boy, she must be a wonderful person."

"She's the best in the entire world. Mrs. Mull, do you mind if I take your daughter to the movies?" Bill asked.

"I guess so since she's been sitting here waiting all day for you to show up. It will take her off of my hands."

She turned to Judy and said, "Eat some popcorn for me. Have fun."

As they got in the truck, Bill said, "Your Momma is really nice."

"Well, what did you expect?" she asked.

"I really didn't know. I was scared to death she'd be just like my English teacher or something," he admitted. "I don't think that woman has smiled since she was a little kid. She scares the devil out of me."

Judy asked, "What are we going to see?"

"I don't remember the title, but Fabian and Tuesday Weld are the stars," he said.

"Is it *High Time*?" she asked.

"That's it," he answered. "I couldn't remember the name."

That's wonderful! How did you know I wanted to see that one?" she said, slapping him on the arm. "I had no idea, but it's the only thing showing at the drive-in," he answered, honest to a fault. "I didn't even check the other theaters."

Bill paid at the entrance and headed straight for the parking space they'd had before. When he turned off the engine, she decided to take him to the concession stand. While standing in line and looking around, Bill asked, "Should we get your Momma some popcorn?"

"No, silly. She was just teasing," Judy said.

"Let's surprise her," he suggested.

Judy looked into his eyes, "I love it. She won't know what to say."

On the way home, Judy said, "I have some bad news. Mother and Daddy have us doing something every single day the rest of the week."

"Oh no. You've got to go with me Friday night. It's an Elvis movie," he protested.

"I can talk my brother into that. Mother's already said it's okay for me to go to the canteen on Saturday night." Judy said, nodding.

"When you give the popcorn to your Mom, tell her it's a thank you from me for letting us go to the canteen," he suggested.

"I can't wait to see her face," Judy said with a chuckle. "Daddy's always the one that gets everyone's attention. Bill, you never fail to surprise me."

"Is that good or bad?" he asked.

"Guess we'll have to see," she said.

Bill was apprehensive on the way to Judy's on Friday evening. Without any contact from her since Monday, he wasn't sure Judy would even be able to go to the movie. He realized he'd worried for nothing as she raced to meet him. When they got to the Swan, Judy saw the sign and turned to Bill, "It's an Elvis movie, huh? Oh really? I think I know why you really wanted to see this movie. Could it be because it's a story about the army, *G I Blues*? You really do want to be a soldier, don't you?"

He smiled, "You know me too well."

"Yeah, but I still like you," she said settling down into her seat.

By this time, they had a routine down. It had become their little ritual to park in the same location and then head to the concession stand before watching the movie.

It was familiar and it comforted him as he knew she would always remember her visits home. Saturday night was a little hard on both of them.

It was the last night they'd be together for a while.

When they entered, they were immediately surrounded by Judy's friends. That didn't stop Bill from pulling her away every time a slow dance came on. It was important to him that they dance every single one of them together. As they walked off the floor after the third dance, Ryan was waiting for them. Bill almost panicked.

Ryan spoke up before Bill had a chance to prepare Judy, "Did Bill tell you we're going to be roommates at NGC?

We're also going to be Second Lieutenants in the army."

Judy showed no reaction to his comments. She just shook her head and said, "So he even convinced a football player to become a soldier?"

Ryan laughed, "You're right, but I sure am glad he did."

Later on her brother's porch, Bill pulled her close and admitted, "Judy, I don't want to let you go. I'll be completely lost without you. What am I going to do?"

She whispered, "Don't you think I feel the same? We'll just have to figure it out together." She kissed him goodnight and walked quickly into the house.

Chapter 46

Bill was on Cloud 9 when he woke up. He'd just had the best week of his life and decided he'd earn as much money as he could so he'd be ready to take her out when she came back up to Blue Ridge again.

His parents were on the front porch talking after church when Bill overheard is Momma ask his Dad, "Sweetie, what's wrong? You haven't been yourself for a couple of weeks."

His Dad paused briefly before answering her, "Honey, I think it's time we got out of the cattle business. I've barely broken even the last two years. The guys at work say the prices are going to be even worse this year. One of them sold all of his cows after losing money last year. I was thinking maybe we should do the same while people are still buying cows and heifers."

Roxanne looked over at him, surprised at how much it seemed to be bothering him. She decided to try to lighten his mood by asking, "Tell me again what a heifer is."

He shook his head in frustration, "It's a young cow before she's had her first calf. Prices are usually a little better for them." He knew he'd told her this before, but he decided not to pursue it.

She just looked at him and reassured him, saying, "Sweetie, do what you think is best. You always make the right decision for us."

He nodded, "Then the sooner the better. If I wait, I'll be competing with everyone else once they get desperate." He handed her his cup and said, "Think I'll go over and see Frank Wright. I bet he'll be willing to buy a few of them."

Roxanne was pleased. Charlie was doing something to solve his problem. She smiled to herself.

Bill had heard every word. He realized his parents had been keeping Roy and him from even suspecting the Carpenter family was in trouble. He realized at that moment he needed to make money, but to save for the family – not going to the movies. After all, it was his responsibility, too. He wasn't a little kid anymore. Warriors didn't hide behind their problems, they fixed them.

Roy walking into the tool shed gave Bill an idea. "Roy, want to go on another treasure hunt?"

Roy wasn't as enthusiastic this time. He thought about it for a moment and then Bill baited the hook by saying, "This time you're not beating me. I'm going to show you how to find the most."

The challenge was all it took. Roy was in. "Can I get some more of those half dollars?"

"How many do you want this time?" Bill asked him.

Unsure he wasn't being unrealistic, Roy asked hesitantly, "How about three?"

"Okay, that's the goal then," Bill agreed. "In fact, if you beat me again, I'll give you the fourth one."

Roy didn't hesitate, "Can we go now?"

"Nah, let's wait until tomorrow. We'll go after breakfast and Momma will think we're playing in the meadow," Bill suggested.

Charlie came in while Roxanne was cooking, "How did it go?" she asked.

Charlie looked relieved, "Great. Frank wants all three heifers and four of the calves. I told him when I sell all of them he could have the hay from our meadow. He said he knew three other guys who were looking to buy. His brother, Gene, is one of them. He volunteered to check with them to see how many they might want next week. Sweetie, we could be out of the cattle business by the end of August."

Just as she started to speak, Bill and Roy came in the back door. She turned to Charlie, hugged his neck and whispered, "That's wonderful." Then she turned to the boys, "Go wash up for supper."

Later Charlie and Roy went into the living room and turned on the television to watch World of Disney.

When Bill heard the song *"When you wish upon a star"* he went in and sat down with them. Roxanne scolded him, "Bill, that cow's not going to milk herself." She tried not to laugh as she watched him slowly back out of the room with his eyes still glued to the set.

Monday morning, Roy almost gave away the treasure hunt to his Momma, when she asked, "What on earth has you so wired up?"

Bill glared at Roy and interjected, "We're going to find some fairy crosses for Ryan."

"Ah, that's nice, but you boys watch out for snakes," she cautioned.

Once outside, Bill started down towards the meadow and Roy called out, "Where are you going?"

"We've got to go find those fairy crosses first," Bill snapped back at him in frustration.

"Why?" Roy whined.

"Cause I told Momma that's what we were doing," he replied. "And like Daddy says, 'Carpenters don't lie.'"

Within minutes, Bill had two fairy crosses in his pocket. Then they headed to Highway 5 to begin their search. By midafternoon they'd found fifteen bottles.

The next day Bill told Roy, "Okay, buddy. Today our goal is to find sixteen of them."

Roy whipped around and looked at him with the funniest expression on his face.

Bill just burst out laughing when Roy asked, "Okay, but what's a goal?"

"It's a measurement on achieving a task," said Bill. "Like you have a goal to get three half dollars as payment when we finish what we're doing."

Roy grinned and started walking again, "I like goals."

"Me, too. Let's make one every day until we manage to make you that money," Bill said.

By the end of July, they had earned Roy four half dollars and twelve dollars for Bill's emergency fund.

Chapter 47

For the rest of the summer, Bill went to the canteen every week. Betty Lou and Jane would ask if he'd heard from Judy the first few times, but they later stopped. It was obvious to anyone who knew him that having to admit he hadn't heard from her was painful. Towards the end of the summer, Ryan started coming. The second time he showed up, Bill handed him the two fairy crosses he and Roy had found.

"What did you do to get these good luck charms?" Ryan asked.

Finally Bill said, "Hey, we need all the luck we can get in order to get into NGC."

"You've got that right, buddy. My grades aren't stellar," Ryan laughed, shaking his head.

It wasn't until October that Bill heard from Judy.

Dear Bill,

I kept waiting for good news before I wrote, but I still don't have any. Daddy is so involved in the church, we don't have any family time at all. My brother comes down to see us, so we have no reason to come up there. I'm so sorry that we can't get together. Mother keeps telling me if we are meant to be together, it will work out. Write me and tell me how the gang at the canteen is doing. Miss you,

Judy

October was turning out to be the busiest of Bill's life. He had a full class schedule as he'd decided to take French instead of a second year of Latin. His instructor hadn't done a great job of preparing the class for the next year's work. She had come in during the middle of the year and had just reviewed what they'd already learned.

Ryan had taken the lead in getting them into NGC. Bill didn't know how Ryan had come up with the list of the requirements necessary in order to even apply, but he was impressed. It appeared to be complete. The first step would be taking the SAT and Ryan's father was taking them to Young Harris College on Saturday to do exactly that. Bill couldn't believe how excited Ryan's dad was about his son going to college.

Like Bill's Daddy, Ryan's had quit school before they'd even gotten to high school and had been forced to work on the farm in order to support the family. On the way, Bill studied every requirement on Ryan's list. One really got his attention – tour NGC and attend a college interview.

The thought of that scared him to death. What on earth would they be expecting him to say? He folded it and carefully put the list in his pocket. He took a deep breath and decided to focus on one thing at a time and maybe he'd get through the process. Everything on the list was in the exact order in which it needed to be completed, so he'd take the SAT and then worry about the next task tomorrow.

A week later, Ryan, Bill and three other students were called into the principal's office. Mr. Dunn smiled, "Boys, you did our school proud. All of you received an outstanding score on the SAT. That means you can apply to any college in the state. Mr. Harper, you have the highest score. That qualified you to be our star student this year. Congratulations." Everyone sat silent as he continued, "Good work. Now get back to class. Congratulations and I'm truly proud of each and every one of you."

On the way back to class, Ryan asked, "Why don't girls have to take that test?"

Bill laughed, "Ryan, remember the blonde you were making eyes at in the seat next to you on Saturday? I'm pretty sure she was a girl."

Ryan blushed, "And a beautiful one, too."

Chapter 48

It was almost Thanksgiving and Bill just knew he'd get a letter telling him Judy would be up for the holiday. But it came and went without a single word. He'd tried to write her, but had no idea what to say and just gave up. Telling her he missed her was all he could get on the paper. There wasn't even a way he could go see her. The only thing left that he enjoyed was spending times with his friends at the canteen. He usually went with Ryan and they took turns driving.

After Christmas, Bill began to see a change in Ryan. He didn't have much to say at all unless they were in the group. Then he'd go on and on about leaving for NGC. Bill was puzzled as he and Ryan had already discussed this all the time at school. Then one night, it was like a light bulb went off – Ryan was trying to impress Betty Lou. After it became clear what was happening, Bill had a ball just sitting back and watching the romance struggling to unfold before his eyes. Finally, he took pity on his friend and said, "Ryan, why don't you just ask her out?"

Ryan whirled around and asked, "Ask who?"

"Betty Lou," Bill said shaking his head. "Did it take you this long to ask out Judy when you guys were dating?"

Ryan hesitated and then admitted, "No, actually she asked me."

"Really?" Bill was shocked. "Are you kidding me?"

"Mother's family goes to the church in Morganton where her Daddy was pastor and that's how we met," Ryan quickly explained.

Bill had always assumed Ryan was comfortable around girls, but he now saw his friend in a new light. He was as shy as Bill.

The first Saturday in January Bill and Ryan were at the canteen. They'd been there for around an hour before a slow song came on. Ryan nudged Bill's shoulder and said, "Well, here goes nothing. Wish me luck." Then he quietly asked Betty Lou to dance with him. When it was over Ryan returned to stand by Bill and grinned, "Can you find a way home? I'm taking Betty Lou home in a few minutes."

Bill nodded and said, "Congratulations, buddy. It's no problem as I see Jimmy on the other side of the room.

I'll ask him or I can always hitchhike. Don't worry about me. Just enjoy the time with your new girlfriend."

"Thanks," Ryan said as he turned and walked to sit next to Betty Lou.

A week later the two boys were invited to an interview at NGC. Ryan's Dad insisted on taking them, which pleased Bill's parents immensely as Charlie didn't want to have to miss work.

Bill knew in addition to that it probably was also due to the cost of the gas it would take to make the long trip. That really worried him because if he actually got accepted, how on earth would his family find the money to pay for tuition? Suddenly he had mixed emotions about even attending as he just knew he wouldn't be able to afford to go. He had less than eight months to come up with the money and finding Coke bottles wouldn't be nearly enough. On the way to the interview, both boys remained quiet. Ryan's Dad realized they were scared. He was so proud of them, but knew they weren't in any frame of mind to hear how he was feeling.

Bill signed in and was taken to a small office and introduced to Mr. Holmes. "Bill, looks like you're a mountain boy. Have you always lived in Blue Ridge?" he asked.

"Yes, sir. Both of my parents are from there as well," Bill answered earnestly.

"I'm a mountain boy, too. I was born and raised in Ellijay. I went to NGC myself. My classmates used to tease me and call me Mountain Goat. Tell me, Bill. Why do you want to come here?" He asked as he sat back in his chair and waited for Bill's response.

"Sir, I've always wanted to be a soldier. My Daddy was in WWII, my Uncle Max served during the Korean War and I have more respect for both of them than anyone I know." Bill explained.

"That's great. It's a long, hard road to becoming a Second Lieutenant, but well worth it. I speak from experience. Tell you what, let's go take a little tour of the campus," he said as he ushered Bill out of the office.

They walked downstairs and started in the mail room. "One of these boxes will be assigned to you."

Then he started walking again, looked back and said, "Let me show you what the best thing is on this floor. This is where you'll get your uniforms. You'll wear one every day as a student here. Do you have any questions?"

Bill stuttered a little, "How much will they cost?"

"Somewhere between $200 to $350. The good thing is that's all you'll need and you can wear the same ones all four years," Mr. Holmes explained. He returned Bill to the entrance and said, "You should hear from us in the next four weeks. Good luck to you and Congratulations."

Bill already knew what tuition was, but the uniform expense was a surprise. He worried about that all the way home."

During the first week of March, his mother handed him a letter from North Georgia College. He ripped it open and began to read. By the time he got to the second page, his mother was asking, "Well, what does it say?"

"It says I'll need two army wool blankets to go on my bunk. Momma, where can I find them?"

"Mull's Department Store," she said eagerly. "Guess that means they accepted you for the fall quarter?"

"Yeah, it's great. Can't wait to tell Uncle Max," Bill said with a huge grin.

She frowned, "What about your Daddy?"

"Momma, I don't think he cares that much about me going to college," Bill said earnestly.

She was hurt that Charlie had made him feel that way.

The next day at school, he sought out Ryan. Before he could say a word, Ryan asked, "Did you get your letter? I did!"

"Yeah, I got it. Guess we're going to college," Bill said proudly. It still didn't seem real to him.

"Guess what? I was talking to some of the football players and Nolan Brookshire told me the plant hired college students during the summer months. We should try to get on there. I bet they pay a lot more than anyone else," Ryan said.

"What do we have to do?" Bill asked.

"I'm not sure. Guess we can get one of our Daddy's to ask," Ryan answered.

That bothered Bill and he worried for the rest of the day about how he'd approach his Daddy. When he got home, he told his Momma what Ryan had suggested. She could tell he didn't want to approach Charlie, so she did it for him.

When she mentioned it to him, Charlie just shrugged, "I'll ask Happy Hill tomorrow."

Bill didn't say a word during the entire meal.

At the canteen later that week, Bill watched Ryan and Betty Lou. He was envious of their obvious attraction. When a slow song came on, he stepped up to ask Betty Lou to dance. "I guess I'm off the hook about taking you to your prom this year," he teased.

She just smiled, "Do you mind?"

"No, you know I think you two are great together. I just wanted you to know it's okay with me."

She was pleased with his response, so immediately asked, "Have you heard from Judy?"

He shook his head, "Guess she's found herself a new fella."

"I thought you two made such a perfect couple."

He just danced in silence for a moment and then said, "I did, too. Guess we just weren't meant to be together."

She felt so badly for him, she rushed to reassure him, "I bet you two get together one day. Just give it some time."

"It'd be nice, but we'll have to wait and see," he said quietly as he looked over her shoulder in thought. The song ended and Bill took her back to Ryan, "Buddy, you better take good care of her. She's a keeper."

Chapter 49

The Saturday after graduation, Jimmy stopped by around noon, suggesting they go meet some of their classmates at the boat dock at the lake. On the way, Bill confessed, "Papaw and Mamaw used to take me to Snake Nation or Dry Branch to fish. She'd fish with me near the small streams coming into the lake, but Papaw always moved around a lot looking for bass. On a good day, he might catch one. Mamaw would catch more than a dozen brim." He laughed and continued, "On a bad day Papaw wouldn't even get a bite and Mamaw would catch her usual amount."

Jimmy laughed, "She sounds like my Mamaw. Wonder how they got so smart.

Bill agreed, "It's crazy cause both of mine are smart."

At the lake they couldn't believe how many people were there. Jimmy had to park on the side of the entrance road. As they walked towards the dock, they saw a group of West Fannin students from all grades. Some were swimming, but one boy was water skiing and that fascinated Bill.

He made it look so easy gliding back and forth the waves with seemingly little effort. Bill decided right then and there he wanted to learn how to do that one day.

When the boat dropped the skier back at the dock, Bill realized it was one of his friends, Ray Stillwell.

It was Ray's father driving the boat. Ray climbed on the dock and Mr. Stillwell left with another skier. It looked like they went towards Morganton Point and then came back. He looked over at Ray, "You were looking pretty good out there for a country boy."

"It's like riding a horse, but doesn't hurt as much when you fall off. You want to give it a try?" Ray asked.

"Nah, don't have my trunks with me. Maybe next time, but thanks." Bill said. No way would he admit to anyone he didn't know how to ski, nor did he plan on learning in front of the entire high school.

He and Jimmy sat on the end of the dock and watched the show. Very few were as skilled at it as Ray had been.

Some fell just a few feet from the starting point. Some guys started betting on how long people would be able to stay up. Bill shook his head at their antics, grateful he wasn't out there.

Roxanne was finishing up the lunch pails for Bill and Charlie early on Monday morning. She put a slice of apple pie in Bill's with a note telling him good luck. Nothing was said between the Carpenter men on the drive to Copperhill. When he parked the truck, he pointed to a little brick building located near the entrance to the plant. "Go over there and check in. When you get off this afternoon, I'll meet you at the truck. Give them a good day's work, son," he instructed Bill.

As he walked towards the building, he saw Ryan and Nolan Brookshire walking to the front door. Several other students were already inside when they entered. Bill knew a few of them, but didn't recognize others. He assumed they attended Copper Basin High School. Two older men were standing in front of the group and each of them began to call out names. Bill, Ryan, Nolan and two other students were called out first.

The older men moved to the door and told them, "Follow me, men." It was the first time Bill had ever been addressed as a man. He liked it. He stood a little taller as he walked towards what the man had called the changing house.

Their leader had them leave their lunch pails in the changing house. Two other men quickly joined their group. They walked back to the main gate and went across to the railroad yard. Stopping in front of a box car, Bill noticed a large pile of dark colored sand. The leader explained, "One of the box cars was overloaded and they'd had to pile the excess on the ground. Our job today is to load this zinc onto the box car. Grab a shovel, men, and let's get to work."

It took the entire day, but they managed to finish their task a little before quitting time. Bill looked around in satisfaction – he was pleased with his day's work.

The labor gang had a new assignment every day. Bill decided they'd be called missions if he were in the army.

He loved that he was seeing the entire workings of the plant for the first time. One week they went to the smelter section, where the copper was melted and processed. Their mission was to clean up the trash and keep everyone safe by making sure the area was clear.

Bill couldn't believe how hot the furnace was and that the men who did that job endured it all summer long. It would be nice in the colder weather as they could stay warm, but summer would be sweltering. It suddenly hit him why there was always several men standing next to the Coke machine. The price was six cents per bottle and he wondered how much change they had to come to work with in order to quench their thirst. After a few weeks he was used to the routine of his gang working all the different sections. It was exciting because every week was different. The only thing that was repetitive was the task of digging ditches for new pipelines. After a month, he was comfortable with everyone. Alvin would pair guys up each day and on this particular day he and Nolan were together. Bill had been dying to know why Nolan ate lunch and then ran outside and went behind the changing house. As he threw a shovel of dirt onto the wheelbarrow, he asked, "Nolan, I know you football players do some crazy things, but what do you do when you run outside at lunch?"

"I'm enrolled at school at Mercer. That's why I qualify to work here, but I really want to go in the Air Force.

I want to be an Air Commander. When I took my physical last month they told me I needed to lose fifteen pounds. The next class is three months away, so I've got to get rid of the weight or they won't take me," he explained. "Every day I eat my lunch and then go outside and throw it up. Believe it or not, it's working. I just have ten more pounds to go."

"I want to be a soldier, but at 157 pounds I don't need to lose any more weight," Bill said, frowning.

Nolan laughed, "You're a lucky man."

As they worked, Bill thought about Nolan's dilemma. Those fifteen pounds helped him be one of the best players on the high school team and now he had to get rid of them in order to get in the Air Force. It dawned on him that of all the students at West Fannin, he and Nolan had more in common than any he knew.

Alvin started the week telling them they'd be cleaning up a mess. "I think they've put it off waiting for you young guys to take care of it. It's a good cause, as they need space cleaned so they can build the new lab."

At the site, Bill immediately visualized what needed to be done. It must have been the place where the entire plant threw their trash. As the day went on, he picked up more trash than he'd ever dreamed of seeing. He swore to himself that he was going to buy a good pair of work gloves. Just before lunch, the boys speeded up, quickly throwing trash and lumber onto the old truck.

Just as Bill was pushing a long piece of metal onto the truck, someone threw a large piece from the side and it landed on Bill's left wrist. Feeling a sharp sting, he looked down and saw he had a two-inch cut. He placed his hand on the cut and yelled out, "Anyone have a clean rag?"

Alvin walked over to see what the problem was and said, "Son, that's going to take more than a clean cloth." He turned to second in command and said, "Sonny, take care of the men while I take Bill to the hospital."

When Bill heard that, he was shocked. His Mamaw had doctored cuts much worse. Why on earth were they sending him to the hospital? He objected, "I don't need to go. Just give me something to keep the dirt out."

Alvin grinned, "Don't have a choice. Company requires me to take you."

Reluctantly, Bill nodded and followed Alvin. He'd heard about the new hospital, but he'd never seen it. It surprised him to see how large and modern it was – like something he figured would be in Atlanta. After four stitches, he returned to work. That afternoon when he was in the truck on the way home his Daddy looked over and asked, "That cut hurt?"

"No, Daddy. They sure made a big fuss about it though."

"They have to. The union people would raise Cain if they didn't," his Dad explained.

Bill was surprised the next day when nothing was said about his injury.

When he cashed his paycheck on Friday, he couldn't believe his eyes. With this money he had enough to pay his first quarter's tuition. He did some more math and realized if he worked until the last week in August, he'd have enough left over to buy his uniforms. He rubbed his hands over the two army blankets his Mom had gotten for him.

He sat down on the bed and thought about how lucky he was and who he could tell about it. It was obvious, Ryan was the one. He'd be the only person who'd appreciate his success. It was hard to fall asleep that night as he couldn't wait to see Ryan at the canteen to let him know college was back on.

Ryan and Betty Lou came in and Bill waited patiently until he had an opportunity to talk to Ryan alone. "Guess what, buddy? With my paycheck from yesterday I have enough for the first quarter's tuition at NGC."

That got Ryan's attention and he grinned, "Really? I just put mine in Daddy's old cigar box."

Bill blurted out, "Daddy stopped smoking a long time ago and I'm glad."

Ryan just nodded, "Yeah, I wish mine would, too."

"You know if we work until the end of August, we'll have enough to pay for the uniforms, too." Bill suggested. But before Ryan could respond, Betty Lou returned and dragged him onto the dance floor.

Bill didn't get to tell Ryan what he was really the happiest about – because he'd worked at the plant his parents wouldn't have the burden of paying for his college for the current quarter.

At lunch the next week, Nolan sat across from him. He didn't say much while they ate, but just kept smiling. After they finished eating, Bill waited for him to get up and go outside as usual, but he didn't move. Suspicious, Bill asked, "Okay, Nolan. What's going on?"

"I've lost 16 pounds and can pass the physical now," Nolan said with a huge grin.

"Congratulations. You did it a lot faster than I ever thought you'd be able to," Bill said.

"Me, too. I managed to do it and now I won't need to put my finger down my throat anymore." Both boys laughed.

Nolan wasn't in the labor gang the next week. By the end of the week, he assumed his friend had joined the Air Force.

Chapter 50

After a month at NGC, Bill realized he knew exactly what his Papaw had always meant when he said he felt like he was in **H*og*-*Heaven*.** No, he hadn't found a large mud hole, but he did get to wear a uniform every single day and every Wednesday he got to either march or play war games. He'd had no idea what he'd major in until he sat through his first math class. It was being taught by the head of the department, Dr. Wicks. He began the class with his concern on our math based on ten. He felt it would be better to be based on twelve. He compared it to the twelve months. Bill was so impressed with the new concept. He'd always thought his Fannin math teacher was smart, but he couldn't pass that knowledge on to his students. Dr. Wicks was so good, he just stopped you in your tracks and really made you think. Bill knew immediately math was his destiny.

He couldn't wait to tell his Momma that every Sunday morning his company commander would march the entire group to downtown Dahlonega to attend church. Looking around his room, he also knew his Momma would love how his room looked.

Those army blankets she'd bought him were tight on the bunk with perfect hospital corners; and yes, Bill Carpenter was in **Hog-Heaven**.

Bill decided to hitchhike home for Thanksgiving break. That way his parents wouldn't need to come pick him up. He looked at his watch to see what time he began his trip and he saw it was noon. He hadn't walked more than two hundred yards down the road when a farmer picked him up. The ride took him to the highway that headed to Amicalola Falls. He got out and started walking. He got another fifty yards and another farmer stopped. He was headed to the falls. Instead of stopping there, he continued on until the intersection at Ellijay to drop Bill off. As the old man drove off, he reminded Bill of Santa as he waved and yelled, "Good luck son. Happy Thanksgiving."

He started walking uphill and noticed all the dead kudzu on both sides of the road. This time a dump truck with Lance written on the side stopped, and asked where he was headed.

"Blue Ridge, Sir." Bill replied.

"Guess what? That's where I'm headed. Get in," said the driver with a big grin.

They talked about Blue Ridge all the way home. When the canteen came up, Bill was surprised the driver was a Korean War vet. He told Bill how proud he was that the VFW let them use their hall to hold their dances. The driver enjoyed the trip so much he detoured and took Bill to the city limit sign on the new highway to West Fannin. Bill thanked him and got out. He got another ride almost immediately.

When he got out near his home, he checked his watch and couldn't believe it was just 2:25 p.m. He ran the rest of the way home.

The time until Christmas passed quickly. Getting ready for finals seemed a lot harder than it had in high school. Bill was apprehensive about getting his grades, so he stayed as busy as he could over the holiday. The first week he was home, he decided to go down to McCaysville to see what was playing at the theater after stopping at the Tastee Freeze where he was going to get a burger and fries. He parked and walked up to the door and there sat Nolan Brookshire in his Air Force uniform.

"Nolan! I guess you passed your physical. Did you get the job you wanted?" he asked.

"Not exactly. We had a career day in basic. I kind of knew the Air Commandos were mostly delivering supplies and supporting rescue and aircraft, but I was impressed by the Air Police K-9 recruiters. After basic I requested that and got it. I went to AP school and when I finished training, they gave me Apache, a German Shepard." Nolan said with enthusiasm.

Bill just grinned, "I guess you like it?"

"I can't believe how much. It took a while for Apache to like me. I sat all day long for days just reading a book next to her before she'd even let me touch her."

"Did it work?" Bill inquired.

"Oh yeah. Now I'm the only one she'll let near her."

"That's exciting," Bill agreed.

Nolan said, "Yeah, it really is, Bill. I just love it."

"When do you go back?"

"Next week Apache and I will go to Guam," Nolan said.

Bill couldn't believe it. Guam? He just said, "I'm jealous."

"Why?"

"Because you're already a soldier and it's going to probably take me a couple of years to get there," Bill explained.

"You'll get there. Just be patient. If I don't see you again before I leave, good luck." Nolan held out his hand.

"You too. Take care of Apache," Bill said.

"That's my job."

Chapter 51

Winter quarter was unlike any other. He didn't like that he couldn't pay any of the tuition and he knew what a burden it was on the family. He also knew instinctively that his Daddy would never say anything about it. He also was disappointed they weren't doing the army games on Wednesday mornings anymore because it was winter. They still made them attend classes on Saturday mornings. He made up his mind he'd study harder this quarter. In addition to the five classes he was taking, he had two additional labs in the evenings. It was eating him up that this quarter was more school than army and he knew he needed some Blue Ridge time.

Both times he planned to hitchhike home, it snowed. He justified his disappointment by studying harder so maybe he'd get a couple of A's on his grades.

The quarter seemed to drag on forever. Two thirds of the way through, he made a life-altering decision. He was going to join the army in the spring. He'd be 19 so he wouldn't need his parents' permission. The more he thought about it, the more comfortable he became with his decision.

If Nolan had been able to get such a good job in the Air Force, he should be able to get an even better one in the Army. Studying helped; he got an A in math and an A in physics.

Later in the spring on a Monday, Bill waited patiently until Roy had left for school. He took a deep breath and said, "Momma, I've decided I'm going to join the army in a couple of weeks."

Roxanna turned around slowly to look at her eldest son, "When did you decide that?"

"A few weeks ago. I really don't like college and it costs too much for Daddy anyway. Are you mad?"

"No, why would I be mad?" she said carefully.

"I guess because I didn't ask you guys first. Do you think Daddy will be mad at me?" Bill asked.

"Son, we've known for years you wanted to be a soldier. If you follow your dreams, we can never be mad. Just make sure you tell your Daddy before Roy does," she cautioned.

Bill's eyes got big, "You're right about that. Roy just can't keep a secret."

When he told his Daddy he was surprised at the response. Charlie said, "Son, can you wait until the first week of April? It's the opening of trout season. That way me, you and Roy can go fishing together. It might be a long time before we'll be able to do it again."

Bill could see the tears welling in his Daddy's eyes and he was touched. "You know, that's a great idea. Can you tell him? He probably won't believe me."

"Bill, he believes everything you tell him, but I will talk to him about going fishing." Charlie grinned.

Bill looked at the calendar and saw the first of April was on a Sunday. He knew there was no way his Daddy would go fishing on a Sunday so they planned for the following Saturday. When they got to Curtis Switch, Roy had everything he needed in his hands. He jumped out of the truck and sprinted to his Daddy's favorite fishing hole at the base of the big poplar. By the time they got there, he'd already caught his first trout. He held up his stringer, saying "Look Daddy at how big it is."

While he was telling them, another fish struck his line. Bill just chuckled. It was a good start to a great day. Bill couldn't tell who was more excited, Roy or his Daddy. He moved down about fifty feet and waded out into the middle of the river. His Daddy went upstream and crossed to the other side. Charlie was in the perfect position to watch Roy fish.

By noon, Bill had four and his Daddy had caught a couple. That bothered him a little until he figured out his Daddy wasn't fishing. He was just watching his boys. At noon, Bill moved upstream until he was across from Roy. He yelled across, "How many you got, Roy?"

Roy proudly held up his string and counted, "I've got eight."

His Daddy yelled, "Time to go home."

It was the first time that Roy had caught his limit. The family rule was when one member caught a limit, they all went home. That was usually Charlie, but Bill realized what his Daddy had let Roy win. What was even better was that Roy would never know it.

Bill realized how much he admired his Daddy after seeing a side of him he'd never noticed before.

On the way home he tried to remember if his Daddy had ever done the same for him. He knew about him teaching him to drive the tractor, but he quickly realized his Daddy had been way too subtle for him to realize what he'd been doing on any other occasions.

Chapter 52

There were a lot more people on the bus than Bill had anticipated. They were on their way to Ponce de Leon Recruiting Center in Atlanta. He noticed several from West Fannin High School and from what he could overhear, most of them had been drafted. He studied their faces curiously and could tell some were excited and many were apprehensive. Two of them appeared to be petrified and he just couldn't understand why. It was the adventure of his life and he was ready to get started.

The organization of events was obviously run by the military. They had a system for everything and there were no deviations. The first thing they had was a physical. Two men were dismissed within the first forty-five minutes – one didn't pass the eye test and the other had flat feet. Bill had never heard of flat feet and immediately began eyeing his own, praying he didn't have them. He moved from station to station doing the height, eye, and weight test. One corpsman noticed the scar on his left wrist and immediately directed him into a special room off to the side. In moments a doctor came in and checked his blood pressure.

He asked, "How'd you get that scar on your wrist?"

Bill told him the story about the scrap metal falling on him and how his company had made him go to the hospital. When he stopped, the doctor looked him dead in the eye and asked, "You didn't do it yourself?"

"No, sir! One of the other guys did it, but he didn't mean to," Bill said earnestly.

"Okay, report back to your NCO," the doctor said as he exited the room.

After lunch all of them were placed in a large room where they'd be administered a test to determine their aptitude for particular jobs available in the army. The NCO in charge said, "Gentleman, this test is important. First let me say, no, if you fail it you won't go home, but then you'll only qualify to be infantry and carry a rifle. We need lots of them. Do your best on this test and you might get a better job you actually like?"

The next morning the senior NCO took them into an auditorium and a Major walked to the front. He had everyone stand and raise their right hand.

Then he administered the oath to swear them into the United States Army. Afterwards, he congratulated them and said, "Okay men, you're now soldiers." When he left the room everyone cheered.

Immediately the sergeant yelled, "Attention!" They all rushed to do as they were told. He ushered them outside and loaded them onto two buses. One guy asked the driver, "Where are we going?"

"Ft. Benning, your new home." the driver said.

When the bus stopped in front of the old white buildings, a sergeant boarded and ordered them to exit and stand on the yellow footprints painted on the ground. One of the guys spoke quietly to the man next to him. Immediately the sergeant bellowed, "No one told you to talk! When you get off the bus, give me twenty pushups. The rest of you get off the bus now."

Bill looked around quickly and watched the others as they responded immediately. He loved it. He was now in the Army. Every day he just knew it would be the day they'd start training, but it didn't happen.

One night the First Sergeant came in and had everyone move outside into formation. Then he broke the news that Ft. Benning had too many trainees and they were going to be bused to Ft. Campbell, Kentucky. It was an all day trip that began right after breakfast. They stopped in route at a restaurant in Chattanooga, Tennessee. The army must have warned them they were coming because they had a chow line set up just like on post.

It was seventeen hundred hours when they arrived at Ft. Campbell and were put into formation as the Post Commander, a two-star general, welcomed them to his post. Bill looked around to see that they were standing in front of two old white buildings – he could have been standing at Ft. Benning, as they looked identical. The next morning at oh-five hundred, their day began.

They were told the barracks were built for WWII and hadn't been used since. Their first mission was to clean up, fix up, and make the building livable. It was boring until one of the guys found a wallet under the barracks. It had three dollars in it and an ID card from 1942. Then everyone else began looking for treasures, too.

Shortly thereafter, they learned to march, double-time, shoot a rifle and clean their weapons. Bill had never been happier. The third week he and two others were called to the Company Commander's office. Lt. Tidwell was going to recommend them for OCS – Officer Candidate School. Bill immediately realized he could become a 2nd Lieutenant before Ryan.

Chapter 53

A tall soldier with dark blue eyes stood outside an old wooden door waiting to enter. With his blond hair cut in a G-I haircut he looked too young to be in the army, much less trying to be an army officer. Finally the NCO gave him permission to knock on the door. He quickly responded with three bangs on the door jam. A strong voice commanded, "Come in."

Private Bill Carpenter marched to the center of the room and stopped, came to attention and saluted, "Private Carpenter reporting, Sir."

Colonel Brown returned his salute, "Private, take a seat. Your company commander tells me you want to go to OCS. Is that right?"

"Yes sir. I've always wanted to be a soldier. I decided a couple of years ago that I would like to be a second lieutenant."

All three officers laughed. Carpenter sat up straight in his chair. He couldn't believe he'd blown his interview on the first question.

The Colonel could see the fear on his face, "We're not laughing at you, son, but you may regret that remark after being a lieutenant for a year. We've all been there."

For the first time, Carpenter actually looked at the Colonel. It helped him to relax a little when he realized he was a lot older and looked a lot like his uncle Max. "Oh, I thought everyone that came here wanted to be a second lieutenant."

"Most do, but others have different motivations. That's why we're here. We have a few questions for you. Answer them as best you can, don't be nervous as it's not a test. We just want to know about Private Bill Carpenter. Major Shaw, why don't you start?"

Shaw paused for a few seconds and ask, "Private Carpenter, how much do you weigh?"

"A hundred and fifty-seven pounds sir."

"That's what it says in your record sheet and I see you're six feet one inches tall."

"Yes sir, is something wrong?"

"Nah, but I bet you get a lot of kidding."

"Yes sir, I always have. My Papaw always said I had to jump around in the shower to get wet."

"Do your bunk mates kid you too?"

"Yes sir. They call me string bean or beanpole."

"Does that make you mad?"

"No sir, not really."

"You telling me it doesn't make you a little mad? It's okay to get mad you know."

"When I was fourteen and my Papaw started kidding me about being skinny I used to get mad all the time, but then when I was about sixteen my Mamaw told me a secret. She said when old people liked you they'd joke with you. Papaw kidding me meant he liked me a lot and I never got mad after that."

"What if they don't like you?"

"Where I come from they just don't have anything to do with you. Sometimes they won't even speak to you."

"Where do you come from?"

"A little town in north Georgia called Blue Ridge."

Captain Farmer interrupted, "By God, that's right. I'm from east Tennessee and I sure wish someone had told me earlier about that."

Colonel Brown broke in and asked, "You really respect your grandparents, don't you son?"

"Yes sir. My Mamaw is one of the smartest women I know."

"That says a lot about you. It says here you have a year of college. Why'd you stop?"

"There's really two reasons. First I didn't study as much as I should have and the main reason is I ran out of money. When I dropped out, they were about to draft me so I joined."

The Colonel looked at Farmer and he asked, "What do you want to be a lieutenant of?"

"I was thinking armor. I think I'd like those tanks."

Colonel Brown smiled, "At over six feet, I'm not sure you'll fit in one. I see you were a math major.

I think field artillery would suit you to a tee. I think we have all the information we need. Do you have any questions of us?

"No sir."

"Good. Tell your commander you'll be recommended for OCS." He stood, saluted and stuck out his hand, "Good luck, Private. Report back to your sergeant."

Carpenter stood, saluted, shook the colonel's hand and about faced, almost running out of the room. He was excited and wanted to talk to the other guys, but as soon as the sergeant saw him he said, "Private, fall in. Squad, attention, right face, forward march."

As they marched back to the barracks Carpenter realized it wasn't so special for Sergeant Murray. It was just another detail for him. When they arrived at the company area, he had them fall out and report back to the platoon area. When Carpenter got to his barracks he was excited and wanted to talk to his buddies, but when he walked inside it looked like a beehive had been turned over. He asked, "What's going on?"

One of the guys answered, "Sergeant Mack is pissed about something. We have a barracks inspection at seventeen hundred and if we fail there won't be any weekend passes."

With the inspection and other activities, he quickly forgot about the interview. Three weeks later everyone began receiving their orders for AIT (Advanced Individual Training). He approached Sergeant Mack, "These orders say I'm going to Ft. Sill. What about OCS?"

Surprised, Mack said, "I thought you knew. You have to get an MOS before you even think about going to OCS. Looks like you're going to be a cannon cocker."

"What's an MOS?"

"The army calls their enlisted jobs MOS or military occupation specialties. Similar specialties are divided into fields. 11 is infantry and 13 is artillery. I'm 11 Bush, infantry or a ground pounder, they call us. Like I said, you're going to be a cannon cocker and shoot the big guns."

"Oh, I understand now. Thanks sergeant."

As he walked back to his bunk, Hoyt Queen, one of his old high school classmates came rushing in. "Heard you're going to Ft. Sill. So am I. We can fly out together. I've never been on a plane before."

He returned his grin, "Neither have I. Should be fun."

They arrived in Lawton, Oklahoma a full day before they needed to report in. Hoyt asked, "Bill why don't we stay in a hotel tonight? It may be the last time we get a good night's sleep."

"Your Mother didn't raise any fools."

Hoyt just laughed, "Well, I'm not too sure about my little brother. So it's okay with you? Let's share a taxi to the nearest hotel."

The next morning they again shared a taxi and the driver seemed to know exactly where they needed to go. He stopped in front of building 411. "Boys, this is where you check in. Good luck and don't let the sergeants get you down."

Hoyt looked at Bill and held out a quarter for a tip.

Bill nodded and added his quarter. He handed them to the driver and said, "Here sir. Thanks for the ride."

"That's my honor and I don't take tips from soldiers." He drove away as Bill held the fifty cents in his hand.

An NCO met them in the doorway and asked for a copy of their orders. "Carpenter, you go to the first desk and Queen, you're at desk number five."

Bill noticed the sign at his desk saying A, B, C, and D. He looked over at Hoyt's and it read Q, R, S, T. He whispered, "Guess I'll see you around post. Good luck."

When Hoyt turned to say goodbye, Bill noticed he was a little pale. It made for an awkward moment. "See you later, Bill."

They moved quickly to their assigned desks.

Chapter 54

Bill looked around at the other students in the classroom and wondered if they were as apprehensive as he was. Everyone sat up a little straighter when a tall, skinny NCO walked to the front of the room, "Gentlemen, welcome to OCS prep. In the next eight weeks we'll determine if you're fit to be a Second Lieutenant in the Field Artillery. For the next two months you'll learn how to compute the data needed by the Gun Sections to put steel on the target. This is like your math courses. You'll build on every class you have and when you graduate you'll have a 13 Echo MOS, Cannon Fire Direction Specialist. The brains of artillery. Open your books and let's get started."

Bill's math background helped him to catch on quickly. The first test seemed so simple. When the NCO passed out the test papers he stopped in front of him, "Good job, Private Carpenter, best score in the class."

"Thank you drill sergeant."

That night Privates Payne, Stillwell and Long came to Bill's bunk. Payne spoke first, "Carpenter, looks like this FDC stuff comes naturally to you.

We thought maybe, if you don't mind, you'd help us. We barely passed and we know this was probably the easiest test we'll have."

He looked at them for a minute and said, "Don't know if I can help, but I'm willing to try."

Every night after that he'd go over everything the NCO had covered in class with them. The best part of his mini classes was he was improving too. He felt like a proud parent when they all aced the next test. With each test their confidence grew, but not the first one of them acknowledged his classes were the reason they were doing so well. It was strange but he realized he didn't care. It was the first time in his life he felt needed. In high school and college he'd always been invisible to the other students, but when he thought about it, he realized he'd created that situation himself. He was sure most people thought he was just shy; however, he knew the truth. He just kept his thoughts to himself. His motivation was he never wanted to be embarrassed again like Mr. Galloway had done to most of the freshman class. He couldn't help it that everyone in his family called wasps 'waspers'.

He knew he'd never forget the wicked smile the teacher had when he asked him how he spelled wasper. It was obvious he was just making fun of the way Bill talked. He decided if he didn't say anything, they couldn't make fun of him. But he had to admit the guys didn't seem to mind the way he talked now. He liked the strong feeling of pride he got helping his buddies. He figured Military Officers felt this way all the time.

Training at Ft. Sill seemed easy compared to basic at Ft. Campbell. That is until his platoon was scheduled for Guard Duty. Bill asked Payne, "Have you noticed the change in Sergeant Bennett? He seems so serious."

"Yeah, heard he was in charge of the guard mount. Lt. Mercier is the officer of the day and will be inspecting the guard detail."

"Is Lieutenant Mercier tough?"

"He's a West Pointer and does everything by the book."

"Why's Bennett so worried?"

"If we fail the inspection, we can't go on guard duty."

"Wouldn't that be good?"

"Hell no. They'd have us re-inspected until we pass. Sergeant Bennett would be put on permanent guard duty."

"Are you sure?"

"No, but I don't want to find out. Do you?"

Sergeant Bennett was standing in the back of the classroom when the instructor dismissed them. He snapped, "Keep your seats. Yes, the rumor is true. You have guard duty Friday night. You're the first platoon from the OCS Prep Battery.

Second Lieutenant Mercier will be Officer of the Day and that means he'll be inspecting you Friday evening. He's proud to be the XO of the OCS Prep Battery. In the past he's inspected five platoons and failed two of them. Gentlemen, you do not want to know what happens then. Raise your hand if you have a fresh, starched fatigue uniform ready for guard mount. All but two hands went up. "You two give me a set of your fatigues and I'll take them downtown for a rush job."

He handed out three field manuals and said, "Those of you with starched fatigues use these manuals to make sure all the patches and insignias are properly placed. If it says a half inch, they don't mean a quarter or five-eighths, they mean a half inch. If you find some of them aren't right, bring them to me and I'll take them to the sewing shop tomorrow. Does everyone understand what's expected of them?"

In unison, they replied, "Yes Drill Sergeant."

"Good, fall out and get to work. I want all the fatigues that need work before you go to the mess hall."

Bill whispered to Payne, "I can't believe he's going to the laundry and sewing shop for us."

"I bet one of those platoons that failed the inspection was his. He's right. I don't want to find out what happens if you fail one of those inspections."

At eighteen hundred hours Friday, Sergeant Bennett had the platoon fall out for inspection. His first command was "Parade rest. Come to attention when I come in front of you."

It was apparent he'd done this before. When he got in front of the first man, his eyes started at his hat and moved down to his boots. When his eyes came back up, he snapped the soldier's rifle out of his hand. It was a total surprise to the soldier and because he tried to hold on he nearly fell. There was a lot of snickering from the platoon. Sergeant Bennett's face turned beet red, "If you do that with Lieutenant Mercier, he'll put you straight on the ground. Now you saw what I did. When you see his right hand move to take your weapon, turn it loose."

The soldier who had messed up asked, "What if he drops it?"

Sergeant Bennett grinned, "I'll buy you a beer."

The platoon cheered. Sergeant noticed Lieutenant Mercier approaching and called them quickly to attention. He did an about face, "Sir, the platoon is prepared for inspection."

"Good, Sergeant. Follow me and take notes."

Everyone had been inspected a lot in basic, but they couldn't believe how sharp the Lieutenant was. He was more like a robot than a man.

No matter how quickly the soldiers released their weapons, he caught it with a death grip. He would ask what a particular general order was and if they responded correctly he would move to the next man. When he got to the last one in the squad he turned to Sergeant Bennett and said, "Good work. March them to the guard house."

Lieutenant Mercier returned the Sergeant's salute and returned to the orderly room. Sergeant Bennett had a huge smile on his face and began singing upbeat cadences all the way back to the guardhouse. Somehow in the past hour, he'd become one of the guys – a team member – not a man to be feared but one who had earned their respect.

The platoon didn't have a clue what they were expected to do so they listened as he explained, "We're responsible for three guard posts. You'll walk your post for one hour and then be relieved. Remember your general orders. You will not leave your post until you're properly relieved. If for some reason we're late, you'll just stay on your post. You will draw numbers to determine time and post. Bill drew post number two at oh-two hundred hours.

Chapter 55

The week before graduation they got their new orders. Only half of the platoon got orders for the new OCS class that started in January. Bill and Larry Payne were on them.

Waiting for a standby seat at the Dallas Airport, Bill thought about how he'd tell his family about OCS. He'd planned to tell them how he'd graduated AIT at the top of his class, then he got a cold chill as he remembered how his Daddy always responded to that kind of talk – 'Sounds like bragging to me.' he'd always say. The more he pondered it, he realized telling him he planned to go to OCS in January would probably end in the same result. Finally around 2 a.m. he got a flight to Atlanta. Once there, he took a taxi to the bus station to buy a ticket on the Trailways Bus to Blue Ridge to surprise his family.

Bill was welcomed by Roy in the front yard. Confused to see him there, Bill asked, "Are you out of school for Christmas?"

"Yeah," then he began to bombard Bill with questions.

It was obvious Roy had no clue what being in the army entailed, so Bill just patiently answered the questions. Finally, Roy said, "Exactly what do you do?"

"I figure out how to aim the Howitzer," Bill said.

"How big is it?" Roy said.

He walked over to Roy and held his hand just above his waist saying, "It shoots a bullet this big from here to West Fannin."

Roy's eyes widened, "No way."

"Trust me, little brother, some of them can shoot even farther than that."

"Is the army fun?" Roy asked eagerly. He couldn't believe he had his older brother all to himself and had decided to take full advantage of the opportunity.

Bill just laughed, "It's the best fun I've had in years."

Roxanne came out on the porch and smiled at Bill, "You boys come on in and get washed up. You know your Daddy will want to eat as soon as he gets here." Bill's entire face lit up at the news his Momma was going to feed him. He was really home.

Chapter 56

The first day of OCS was exactly like OCS Prep. He'd been worried about all the rules and they'd been in formation, which meant he couldn't take notes. Lt. Stewart began to brief them, "OCS is six months long. It's broken down into three sections – the first one, which you're currently in, is Blue Birds, then Green Bird and finally Red Bird."

Later Bill would discover Blue Birds had to run everywhere when they were outside. That didn't bother him much, but he did worry that you weren't allowed to walk on north/south sidewalks. That rule applied to the entire post and if you were caught on the wrong sidewalk, you'd be required to do twenty push-ups. The Candidates just looked at each other when this rule was given. How on earth would they know which ones ran north and south and which ones could you actually walk on?

Bill's solution was to not walk on any of them. He thought he was smarter than them until he got to an area marked, 'Keep off the grass.' It was signed by the First Sergeant.

He felt it was unfair until he learned as an Artillery Officer you had to be able to read a map and know where he and his unit were located at all times. Knowing which way was north was the first requirement. The one that really got the attention of the Cadets was that you could never lie.

Getting caught in a lie meant an immediate removal from the program. The scary part of the problem was quibbling was considered a lie. Bill's first encounter with that came while on one of the classroom breaks. One of his classmates asked if he had an extra quarter to buy a Coke. Bill had two quarters, but he never thought of it as having extra. But he was afraid if the Tac Officer had him put his money on the table and saw he had two quarters he could be put out of the program. Keeping that quarter wasn't worth the risk, so he handed it over to his classmate.

Because the rule seemed so vague, all of the candidates were overly cautious. It wasn't until three weeks had gone by that they were given the parameters of the rule. When everyone fell out into formation, the requirement was the last one out of the House had to lock the door. The last one out was Candidate Moore, who was buttoning his shirt as he came out.

As he took his place with the squad, Lt. Stewart yelled, "Candidate Moore! Did you lock that door?"

Moore snapped back, "Yes, sir!"

Lt. Stewart walked over to the door and when he pulled on the handle, it opened. He did an about face, "Candidate Moore, report to the First Sergeant."

Later that day, they discovered he was no longer a Candidate. It was sobering for the remaining candidates. They now understood the rules and were terrified of breaking them.

Bill and Larry were in the back of the classroom a couple of weeks later waiting for the instructor to get there. Bill broke the silence, "My Mamaw was right when she said as long as you stay busy, time flies by. It's hard to believe we're Green Birds, isn't it?

Larry nodded and said, "I agree. The Lieutenant keeps us busy. I wonder sometimes if he ever sleeps. He's in our house every night doing those darn inspections."

The instructor walked in and pulled down a screen. Written in bold, red letters was The Artillery is the King of Battle. He pointed to the saying and said, "Of course, that makes the Infantry the Queen of Battle. Congratulations gentlemen, you've now entered the second phase of OCS. Today's class is teaching you how to be a forward observer, or FO. What does an FO do, you ask? He's the eyes of the artillery. A good one will identify a target, request a fire mission and adjust the rounds to get steel on the target. Many of you will become FO's for our Division Artillery in the 82nd Airborne and 101st air assault. That's just naming two of them. A good FO can identify the enemy's location and quickly adjust, destroying them before they destroy us. Open your books and let's get started."

During the break, Larry said, "I don't want to be an FO. I want to be a helicopter pilot. The First Sergeant told me I can apply when I become a Green Bird. I'm going to see him as soon as we get out of class today. Why don't you go with me?"

Bill thought about it for just a minute and then grinned, "Yeah, why not?"

Bill pulled out his new little goals notebook and made the entry.

My Goals.

1. Be a soldier.

2. Learn how to milk a cow.

3. Learn to dance.

4. Get a White Sport Coat, go to Prom.

5. Become an Army 2LT.

6. Become a Helicopter pilot.

In the orderly room, Bill saw a familiar face. He finally remembered where he knew the cadet. He'd been at NGC in some of his classes. He started to approach him and then noticed he was a Red Bird. Just as he decided not to say anything, the soldier came up to him. "Carpenter, I can't believe it. Do you remember me? My name is Jerry Fink."

"Yes, sir. I remember you, but figured you wouldn't have a clue who I was," Bill said.

"Well, I'm glad we crossed paths. You're lucky, you just got yourself a Big Brother. That's me, so my job is to help an underclassman.

Mine just got his Second Lieutenant bar and went to Ft. Hood, Texas. Which house is yours?" he asked.

"The one across from the mess hall," Bill said.

"When you're finished with the First Sergeant, I'll walk over to the house with you. Are you in some kind of trouble?"

"No sir. I'm here to apply for helicopter school," Bill said proudly.

Jerry laughed, "I can't believe it! That's exactly why I'm here."

Bill was surprised a week later when he returned from a field exercise and found two candy bars under his pillow. He didn't know how Jerry had known he was in the field, but from that point on, he always found candy bars Jerry had left him for his return.

After a couple of weeks as a Green Bird, he accumulated enough demerits to earn a Jark to Signal Mountain and back – a four mile trip. He asked, "What in the world is a Jark?"

Three of the guys laughed, "It's not a run or a march. It's a fast walk. You'll find out pretty quickly exactly what it means."

One of them asked, "Do you have a Big Brother?"

"Yeah, Jerry Fink," Bill said proudly.

"Great, on your first Jark when you get to the top of the mountain, pick up the biggest rock you can find, bring it back and give it to him. He has to sleep with it that night."

"Are you kidding me?" Bill asked incredulously.

"Ask the Lieutenant," the soldier said.

So Bill did exactly that the next morning. He replied, "Cadet Carpenter, who's your Big Brother?"

"Cadet Jerry Fink, Sir."

The Lieutenant just grinned evilly, "Then make sure you get a big rock!"

"I will, sir."

Bill reported to the orderly room for his Jark on Saturday morning.

He felt a little better about it when he realized there were eight other cadets waiting as well. No one was talking. The leader told them to form two lines and fall in, right face and forward march.

Apparently the two cadets in the lead had done this before, as they increased their speed to an extremely fast walk.

It didn't take long until they turned onto a dirt road which led to the top of Signal Mountain. At the top, the leader commanded, "Fall out and take ten minutes."

Bill noticed he wasn't the only cadet looking for a rock. The first one he picked up was about the size of a cantaloupe. Not only was it heavy, but it would be really awkward to carry for a couple of miles. Then he noticed a long, slender rock about fifteen feet down on the backside of the hill. When he picked it up, he knew it was perfect for Fink. He guessed it was about a foot long and six inches wide and it would be easy to carry.

When he was released at the orderly room, he ran to his house. He yelled, "Does anyone have a ruler?"

Cadet Rogers handed him one and Bill was surprised when he measured the rock that it was sixteen inches long and seven inches wide. Two cubicles down Cadet Sanders had a rock. They decided to walk over to the Red Bird house together. Bill figured Fink would be mad when he was handed the rock, but instead he laughed out loud.

"Bill, I can't believe you managed to find an even bigger rock than the one I gave my big brother. I'm impressed." Fink finally got out.

As they walked back, Sanders said, "Hey that was fun."

Bill laughed, "Yes it was. Fink loved it. When I'm a Red Bird, I'm going to be a Big Brother, too."

Sanders quickly agreed, "I think I will too."

Chapter 57

The second phase of training went even faster. Bill was so overwhelmed he forgot to tell Jerry Fink goodbye. He sincerely hoped their paths would cross again someday. Red Birds were the top dogs in OCS and only real officers outranked them. Bill noticed that new status immediately went to some of the cadets' heads. Classes were so much more interesting to him now.

A survey class came next in the program. For about two weeks they learned everything that had to do with the subject. Bill loved it – it was applied mathematics and right up his alley. He hadn't enjoyed a class this much since geometry with Mr. Haymore. When he'd completed the course, he decided it was time to find a Blue Bird who needed a Big Brother.

He studied the formation of Blue Birds first. He was looking for someone from his OCS prep class, but that didn't prove successful. He began to worry he'd never find someone and he only had five more weeks until graduation. Then his luck changed. They had a class located next to a group of Green Birds.

The first cadet he saw was Cadet Stillwell from his OCS Prep class so he approached him after the class. They talked for a few minutes and Bill offered to be his Big Brother. Now he had to find out when Stillwell would be going on field exercises and how he could get candy under his pillow. He approached the Lieutenant with his questions and he immediately helped him with all of the candy runs.

Every weekend afterwards, Bill expected to have to sleep with a big rock. He decided Stillwell must be a fantastic cadet and he hoped his luck would continue. Bill only had two weekends left before graduation.

Monday the Lieutenant talked to the class about graduation, telling them about the tradition of the first salute as a Second Lieutenant. The first NCO that saluted them was to be rewarded with a silver dollar. When Bill heard that, he immediately thought of Sergeant Bennett. Once in the classroom, he told Larry what he'd been thinking. Larry laughed, "I can't believe it. I had the same thought myself. Let's go over and invite him to our ceremony."

They were so excited about it they couldn't wait until the weekend.

As soon as class dismissed, they skipped chow and went straight to see the Sergeant. He was happy to see them and promised he'd attend.

Graduation had finally arrived. Cadet Rogers, who lived two cubicles down had a father who was a General and he showed up for the service that morning. The Cadre was surprised and all of their attention was diverted to the General.

All the cadets had to do was March there and hold up their right hands to be sworn in. Sgt. Bennett was there as promised. Bill nor Larry had silver dollars, so they both gave him two half dollars. Bill was amazed at how great that salute made him feel.

Back at the house the First Sergeant was there to sign them out on leave and give them their new orders. Both were ecstatic. They were to report to Mineral Wells, Texas the second week of July for helicopter school. That gave them three weeks of leave and they'd already made arrangements with another cadet who had a car to get a ride to the Dallas Airport.

As all the events of the day were completed, Bill looked around and couldn't believe the feeling of accomplishment he had and how lucky he felt.

Chapter 58

Bill got more and more excited while taking the Old Highway 5 path home. He opened the back door and walked in, shouting, "Surprise! Your oldest kid is home."

No one answered. He checked all the rooms in the house and no one was there. He started to wonder where they were and then he began to worry. He walked out on the front porch and looked over the farm. He was about to give up when he noticed movement in the meadow. They were hauling hay. That gave him an idea. He went into the room he shared with Roy, took off his uniform and quickly pulled on work clothes. He ran to the meadow. They were so busy they didn't see him until he came around the trailer that was piled high with freshly-cut hay. Needless to say, it was a while before the job was finished.

Two days went by before anyone in his family even mentioned the army. Even Roy seemed more interested in going trout fishing than he did what was happening with Bill.

The following Saturday, Roy got his wish and all three of them were in the river at daybreak.

Just like before, Charlie let Roy win and watched as he caught seven trout. Then Charlie waded out to the middle of the river and started cleaning them. Bill took the hint and began cleaning the four he'd caught as well. By the time they'd finished, Roy had caught his last trout. Bill moved over to where his Daddy was planning to tell him he'd made Second Lieutenant. As he got closer, he began to worry that Charlie would just discount the promotion and say his usual, "Sounds like bragging to me." Changing his mind about telling his Daddy, he decided instead to ask for his help in buying a car. He'd been thinking it was time he drove to his next duty station. He didn't want a new one, just a reliable used one. His Daddy would know who he could trust.

About five feet away from his Daddy, he asked for his help with the car. Charlie smiled, "There's a good guy on Harper Town Hill in McCaysville. He's always been fair with me. I bet he'd give you a fair deal. Let's clean that last fish and take them home. Then, after lunch, we'll go check it out."

Bill was surprised at how quickly his Daddy had offered to help. As they drove up, Bill immediately saw the car he wanted – a two-toned green 1955 Chevy.

The cadet who'd taken him to the Dallas Airport had been driving one exactly like it. His Daddy knew the salesman who approached them, "Jim, my boy needs a car. What have you got?"

Bill spoke up quickly, "How much is that '55 Chevy?"

"I believe it's priced at $600, but let me check with the boss," said Jim. When the owner came out, Charlie recognized him and explained Bill wanted a car to drive to his next duty station. The owner asked where Bill would be driving. Bill replied, "Mineral Wells, Texas."

Charlie said, "The boy was looking at that '55 Chevy. What kind of deal can you give him?"

"How much can you put down on it?" the owner asked.

Bill looked in his wallet and counted his money, "Guess about a hundred. I'll be needing the rest for gas and food on the trip."

"Well, it's listed at $600, but what do you think about $550?

I'll take your hundred and you can pay me $50 a month until it's paid off. What do you think?"

Bill stuck out his hand, "It's a deal."

The owner ushered them inside to give them the paperwork and address to send the money and told him he could drive it home. Charlie smiled in satisfaction, "I'll see you at home, Son."

While dealing with the paperwork, the owner said, "Bill, I've got one of these myself. I need to show you something." They walked out to the car and he said, "The gear shift is on the steering column on the Chevrolet."

He had Bill get in and change the gears a few times until he was comfortable with the procedure. Then he explained the problem, "After a couple of years, the gear shift would lock down. It's an easy fix if you know what to do." He raised the hood and showed Bill the two bearings above the transmission. He pulled out a screwdriver from his back pocket and continued, "When it does it, take a screwdriver and push down on the right gear bearing and it's fixed."

Bill looked at him gratefully, "Thank you, Sir. Daddy said you were a good man and you just proved it to me."

"Thanks, son. Take this screwdriver and put it in your glove box so if you ever need one, you'll have it." He closed the hood and shook Bill's hand, "Good luck in the army. What will you be doing in Texas?"

"Learning to fly a helicopter," Bill said proudly.

"Well that's just great. Promise to come back and tell me what it's like?" he asked with a grin.

"I'll do just that," Bill promised. As he drove away in his new car, the owner waved just like a member of the family would. Instead of going straight home, he checked out the Tastee Freeze in McCaysville, but was disappointed he didn't see a single person he knew. He drove out of the parking lot and headed to the one in Blue Ridge, hoping for better luck. He did the same old cruise from Tastee Freeze to Lance's Drive-In on the north side of Blue Ridge. He struck out again. He guessed all his friends were out of school and had moved away to find work.

Chapter 59

When Charlie left for work, Bill asked his Momma if he could make a long distance phone call. "I'll pay, but I need to call Larry Payne. He lives in Gainesville," Bill explained.

She smiled, "Make your call and don't worry about paying, son."

When he got Larry on the phone, he told him all about his new car, which meant they didn't need to fly to Texas. They would need to leave a little earlier, however. They decided to meet at the traffic circle in Ellijay on Wednesday morning at ten o'clock.

Bill loaded all of his military gear in the trunk of his car the next morning while his Mamma was milking the cow. He decided to also take some of his civilian clothes. When she came back to the house, he broke the news that he was leaving early, explaining how driving would take a lot longer. "I guess I need to go spend some time with Mamaw and Papaw," he said.

She hid her disappointment, saying, "I'm sorry you need to leave so soon, but you know best, son. Spending time with your grandparents will make their day. You can take their milk and butter when you go."

Nothing more was said about Bill leaving until Wednesday morning after Charlie went to work. His Mamma and Roy stood and waved as he drove away.

Larry was waiting in front of the theater with his parents. Their goodbyes were a little awkward for Bill, but they were soon on their way. Checking the maps, he decided the best route was Interstate 20 all the way to Ft. Worth. The first day they made it to the Texas state line before resting. They took turns driving and finally entered the Primary Helicopter Center just before noon on Friday.

At headquarters, they signed in. Looking around they could see it was a one-stop location. The next requirement for them was to find a place to live. They learned the entire town of Mineral Wells was set up just to support the school and when they told the lady they were looking for places, she flipped through her cards.

"I have a perfect place. It's a two-bedroom trailer located just this side of the big hotel downtown."

The next stop for them was finance. They needed their back pay. The clerk counted out their money as cash and told them they'd be getting $700 a month in TDY pay. The just looked at each other and burst out laughing. The clerk was confused, "You guys didn't know about that?"

Bill answered, "No! Why do we get it? I just figured we'd get flight pay."

"Yeah, you'll get that, too. It's because you'll only be here four months, you qualify for TDY pay. You have to be in a location for less than six months in order to get it."

Later when they saw the trailer, Larry spoke up, "What's that thing you keep saying all the time – 'Good Lord looks after fools and country boys?' Guess we qualify in both areas."

Bill laughed, "You're right. We've had a wonderful day."

They were surprised and delighted to see the trailer was set up almost like a motel room and the only thing they needed was to pick up some groceries.

Chapter 60

Today Bill was going to actually fly in a helicopter. His instructor, Mr. Newman, was a quiet man and a civilian. He pointed out the OH-23D they'd be flying that day.

It was a three seater. So Bill, as the pilot, would sit in the middle. Mr. Newman calmly said in his slow, Texas accent, "All you need to do is put your feet on the pedals, your right hand on the stick – or what we call a cyclic. With your left hand reach down and grab the stick that's level with the deck, which we call the collective. That makes you go up and down. On the end of the collective is a throttle, just like the one on a motorcycle. You turn it counter clockwise to add power.

So you see you only have four things to do to fly the helicopter. Today we'll work on the pedals and the collective."

Mr. Newman flew them to an open field and the training began. Bill learned if he moved the pedals the nose would move right or left. After a few days he began to move the nose without even thinking. Next he learned to control the collective and after a couple of weeks he didn't even have to worry about the throttle. He could tell by the sound of the engine if it was right. The cyclic was his biggest problem. It required only small movements and Bill kept making large ones. Mr. Newman counseled him saying, "You're over controlling. Just think where you want to go and relax."

It sounded so easy, but it took Bill days to achieve his objective. After about twenty hours of training, Mr. Newman landed the aircraft on the runway and turned to Bill, "Okay, it's time for you to solo. I want you to take off and fly the traffic pattern three times and then land. Any questions?"

"No, sir," Bill said. He had done this more than fifty times with Mr. Newman in the aircraft, but he was still apprehensive the first time he went up alone. The next two times were fun. That night he bragged to Larry, "I can actually fly that helicopter."

Larry said, "Yeah, it is fun. Guess the hard part's over for us now."

Bill seemed surprised at the comment and then said, "I guess it is."

The next day they found out they were wrong. That's when they were introduced to an Auto Rotation – landing with an engine failure. For the remainder of their time at Ft. Wolters, Mr. Newman would cut back the throttle at least three times during each training flight. Bill didn't realize it at first, but by the time the four months were up Auto Rotation was just another normal exercise.

Bill pulled out his goals notebook and made the entry.

My Goals.

1. Be a soldier.

2. Learn how to milk a cow.

3. Learn to dance.

4. Get a White Sport Coat, go to Prom.

5. Become an Army 2LT.

6. Become a Helicopter pilot.

7. Make the Army a Career!

The first phase of flight school ended just before Christmas. Bill's orders had him reporting to Hunter Airfield in Savannah, Georgia the first week of January. That meant he and Larry could spend Christmas with their families. On the way home, they took turns driving. Bill decided it was easier to just take Larry to Gainesville than it would be to coordinate a pick up point. He didn't tell his family he was coming home because he just loved surprising them. His timing was great. He arrived just in time to help Roy cut a Christmas tree.

Of course, Roy graciously let Bill lug it all the way to the house. On the way, Roy told Bill Santa was bringing him an electric train. Bill asked, "What happened to my train?"

"It's old and some of the tracks don't even work," Roy complained.

"So that's your excuse?" Bill said.

Roy's face turned red and Bill hated that he'd inadvertently hurt his brother's feelings. He said, "Why don't we shoot down some mistletoe when we get home for Momma?"

Two days before Christmas Bill told his Momma, "I need to go see the guy who sold me my car. I have the money to pay it off and I'll feel better once that's done."

"I understand, son. Why don't you take Roy with you? He'll love spending time with you." she suggested.

"He likes riding in my car," he said with a smile at her. When they reached their location, Bill stepped inside to find the owner.

He quickly said, "See? I told you I'd come back. Here's the rest of what I owe you, sir." Bill said sticking out his hand full of cash.

"Thank you, son. Now tell me, what's it like flying that helicopter?"

"It's wonderful. You can do so much more with it than you can with a fixed wing. Thanks again for the car. It runs great." Bill said.

As soon as they climbed into the car, Roy asked, "Can you fly a helicopter?"

"I'm learning. I'm halfway there, but let's keep that between you and me. You know if Daddy hears it he's going to accuse me of bragging again." Bill cautioned.

"That's true, but more importantly, Momma will worry herself to death. I promise I won't tell," he said shaking his head.

The brand new electric train was up and running by the time Roy got up on Christmas morning.

Bill and his Daddy had gotten up before dawn to assemble it in order to surprise Roy. Of course, Momma had to supervise as she was preparing her big Christmas breakfast for her boys.

Chapter 61

It was the first week of January when Bill started his trip to his next duty station – Hunter Airfield in Savannah, Georgia. He picked up Larry in Gainesville and headed I-85 to Atlanta, then I-75 to Macon, and finally I-16 to Savannah. When they were close to their destination, Bill looked over at Larry and said, "You know Daddy always told me Georgia was the largest state east of the Mississippi. Boy was he right. Let's find us a motel and sign in tomorrow."

The sign-in area was set up exactly like the one in Mineral Wells. They were lucky enough to get another two bedroom trailer located just south of the airfield. The two major changes were their IP was a Warrant Officer, CW2 Perry; and the aircraft was a Huey. They were paired off differently the next morning. Bill was paired off with Warrant Officer Candidate Wilson from Valdosta, Georgia. Perry took Bill and Wilson out to the aircraft and showed them how to make a preflight inspection. Then they got inside and received the best news ever.

Perry explained, "When you roll on the throttle to max a governor takes over and makes all the changes on the engine."

What that meant to Bill was he only had three things to worry about now – the pedals, the cyclic and the collective.

Their first exercise for the day was to hover. Bill kept thinking about what Mr. Newman had told him – just think about where you want to go and don't over control. Mr. Perry was impressed with Bill's performance and over the next four months Bill and Wilson got to fly a C Model Huey Gunship, shoot a machine gun and rockets, then they had to practice sling loading a fifty-five gallon drum of water. As the weeks went by, they learned to fly in formation, and to land at night to flashlights set out in a T-formation. The last month of the school they got their orders. As expected, the orders were for Vietnam. The ended their training with an Escape and Evasion course. They ate rattlesnake and prepared rabbits over an open fire.

Then they had to travel miles through the middle of the swamp on Ft. Stewart. The instructors told them Ft. Stewart was really Camp Swampy in the comic pages.

When they returned to Hunter Air field the First Sargent took a class picture for them. Friday morning the class was put in formation for the award of their Aviation wings. It was a short exercise and then Bill and Larry were on their way home.

Chapter 62

Roy had waited until Friday night just before they went to bed to ask Bill just one thing. "Did you learn to fly helicopters?"

Bill grinned and pulled out his brand new aviation wings, "I sure did. They just gave me these wings. Did you tell Momma or Daddy?"

"No way. I promised you I wouldn't," he said earnestly, reaching out to touch the prize.

Bill handed them to him saying, "Good. Here, you can have these and maybe one day you can earn a set of your own. Now go to sleep. I want to be in the river by daybreak."

The morning was exactly as Bill had hoped. His Daddy did as expected and Bill was having the best fishing day of his life. When he got to seven trout, he pretended to continue to fish, but didn't actually have any bait on his hook.

Roy started to brag on the way home about what a great fisherman he was and Charlie cut him short with his usual admonishment, "Sounds like bragging to me. Carpenter men don't brag. They just do."

Roy's face turned red and he apologized. Charlie turned to Bill and winked.

Time flew by for Bill and he couldn't believe twenty days had passed before he even realized it. Two days before he had to return to duty, his family had just sat down to dinner when he asked if they could take him to the airport and keep his car until he returned. His Momma asked, "Where are you going, son?"

He answered, "I'm going to Vietnam as a helicopter pilot."

There was complete silence as they quietly digested what he'd said. Finally, his Daddy asked, "How long will you be there?"

"Just one year," Bill reassured them.

His Daddy smiled, "Just in time for trout season when you get back, son."

Bill smiled, "Yeah, and this time I'm going to beat Roy."

"No way," Roy yelled. "You can never beat me."

Momma said, "You boys quit arguing and eat your supper."

The following morning all four climbed into Bill's car as he drove them to Atlanta. The ride seemed especially long because no one had anything to say. Bill pulled up at the terminal and when he got out his Daddy and Momma followed him.

She gave him a tight hug and returned to the car without opening her mouth. Charlie looked at Bill and said, "Make them a good soldier, son." He nodded at Bill and returned to the car and pulled away from the curb.

Bill bought a ticket because he wasn't sure flying standby would get him to Ft. Dix in time. At 0900 the next morning he was on his way to Vietnam. He was surprised and a little disappointed to see he didn't know anyone on the flight.

Chapter 63

On the first day of April, Bill began packing his duffle bags to come home. He looked over at his roommate who was watching him in amusement and explained, "Mamaw always tells me if you stay busy, time will fly by. I can't believe how fast the last twelve months has gone."

Jerry said, "Bill, you look strange dressed in your khakis. Where are they sending you next?"

"Ft. Sill, OK for the advance course," Bill said proudly. "I have to wear these because I had to turn in all my flight gear. Guess I'm just lucky they still fit. Jerry, I know you're a short timer as well. Where are you headed?"

"Ft. Rucker, AL. I'm hoping to be an instructor pilot," Jerry said.

"Shouldn't be a problem now that you're a CW3," Bill replied.

There was a knock on the door and someone called out, "Bill, the old man wants to see you before you sign out."

"Captain Kerns, give me a couple of minutes and I'll walk over with you," Bill said as he stuck his head out of the door.

He was surprised to see a room full of his fellow pilots when he reached the orderly room. Major West said, "Welcome Captain Carpenter."

Bill shook his head, "Sir, I'm a First Lieutenant."

"You don't argue with your Company Commander, son. No, you're not a First Lieutenant. You've been a Captain for three days. I told the First Sergeant not to tell you until we could do it right. Captain Kerns, read the orders, please."

As Kerns read the orders, Major West pinned on the Captain bars. When Kerns finished, West turned to the First Sergeant, who handed him a medal. "Captain Kerns, read the citation."

As he read it aloud, Bill realized he was being awarded the DFC, or Distinguished Flying Cross.

Major West concluded the ceremony and then asked, "Are you ready to leave?"

"Yes, sir. I just need a ride to the 90th replacement," Bill replied.

"Captain White, is his ride ready?" asked the Major.

"Yes, sir. The maintenance bird is sitting on the pad right now."

"Well gentleman, I guess our next mission is to WET-DOWN Captain Carpenter's new Captain Bars. Let's adjourn to the officer's bar and the drinks will be on our new Captain. Any questions?" chuckled the Major.

After total silence, they left for the bar. For more than an hour Bill nursed his one beer until the money he'd given to the bartender upon his arrival had been used up. He shook hands with everyone there and followed Captain White to the helicopter. His roommate had loaded his duffle and his briefcase onto the bird for him. It was only a thirty minute flight to his destination and Captain White didn't even shut down as Bill exited. As soon as Bill was out of range, the Captain departed.

Bill signed in at the headquarters building and was soon on a bus to Saigon.

After that he entered the freedom bird for the trip to Travis Air Force Base in California. While traveling, he pulled out his 201 File and read the update. He was surprised to see he'd also won an air medal with fourteen awards – one for each fifty hours of flight in a hostile environment.

Then he pulled out his goals notebook and quickly added 'Be a Company Commander of an Aviation Company'. He smiled as he wrote, "Beat Roy trout fishing".

My Goals.

1. Be a soldier.

2. Learn how to milk a cow.

3. Learn to dance.

4. Get a White Sport Coat, go to Prom.

5. Become an Army 2LT.

6. Become a Helicopter pilot.

7. Make the Army a Career!

8. Be a Company Commander of an Aviation Company!

9. Beat Roy trout fishing

He slept for the remainder of the long flight. As soon as he arrived at Travis he took a taxi straight to the airport in San Francisco. He was in uniform when he tried to purchase his ticket. The lady behind the counter helpfully suggested, "Sir, if you'll wait another hour you can fly all the way to Atlanta on standby."

"Thank you, ma'am. That's awfully nice of you," Bill said, touched at her generosity.

She explained, "My husband is in Vietnam right now. It makes me feel good helping other soldiers. Hopefully, someone else is being kind to him."

Bill arrived in Atlanta after midnight and knew he wouldn't be able to take a bus until later in the morning. He quickly decided to rent a car instead so he could be home in a couple of hours. The clerk told him the closest place to return the car would be in Canton. It would be a little out of his way, but he decided getting home was a lot more important.

As he passed through Canton, he saw a 24 hour restaurant and considered stopping to grab breakfast, but then had a better idea.

If he kept driving, he'd get home early enough to be there for his Momma's gravy and cathead biscuits. He was consumed with that thought for the rest of his drive. As he came up the driveway and pulled in behind his Chevy, he parked, got out and ran to the back door. He opened it and yelled, "MOMMA, CAN I HAVE SOME GRAVY AND BISCUITS?"

Made in the USA
Lexington, KY
20 December 2019